FOUNDE

Bet

BEOWULF

A PROSE TRANSLATION
WITH AN INTRODUCTION BY
DAVID WRIGHT

PENGUIN BOOKS

Penguin Books Ltd, Harmondsworth,
Middlesex, England
Penguin Books, 40 West 23rd Street,
New York, New York 10010, U.S.A.
Penguin Books Australia Ltd, Ringwood,
Victoria, Australia
Penguin Books Canada Limited, 2801 John Street,
Markham, Ontario, Canada L3R 1B4
Penguin Books (N.Z.) Ltd, 182–190 Wairau Road,
Auckland 10, New Zealand

This translation first published 1957
Reprinted 1959, 1960, 1961, 1963, 1964, 1965, 1966,
1968, 1969, 1970, 1972, 1973, 1974, 1975, 1976, 1977, 1979,
1980, 1982, 1983, 1984, 1985, 1986

Printed in the United States of America by
Offset Paperback Mfrs., Inc., Dallas, Pennsylvania
Set in Linotype Weiss

CONTENTS

ACKNOWLEDGEMENTS

I wish particularly to thank Mr S. S. Hussey for the assistance and advice which he has given me in the interpretation of crucial passages in the text, in the revision of the final draft of my translation and for his help in the Notes and Appendices; Mr John Heath-Stubbs and Mr George Barker for their criticisms and suggestions; and Mr T. S. Eliot for permission to quote four lines from *East Coker*.

INTRODUCTION

ALMOST everyone has heard of *Beowulf*, which is one of the earliest and indeed the most impressive of the Anglo-Saxon or Old English poems that have come down to us. The whole body of Old English poetry known to be in existence comes to no more than about 30,000 lines; and though it is written in the same kind of verse, the alliterative measure, yet in spite of this uniformity the poetry is astonishingly varied. There are heroic poems like *Beowulf*, *The Finnsburg Fragment*, *Widsith*, *Waldere*, and *The Battle of Maldon*; religious poems such as *Judith* (which is found in the same MS as *Beowulf*), *Guthlac*, *Genesis*, *Exodus*, *Christ*, and *The Dream of the Rood*; and magnificent lyrics and elegiac pieces like *The Seafarer*, *The Wanderer*, *The Wife's Lament*, *The Husband's Message*, and *The Ruin*. These are only a few. There are also a number of short pieces – gnomic poems, riddles, and charms.

Beowulf is one of the longest as well as the most important of complete poems in Old English. It is not a relic of savage bygones, nor is it merely a document of historical importance. It is the only native English heroic epic, and one of the finest products of what used to be called the Dark Ages of Europe. There is also the point – until recently often overlooked – that it is a great poem in its own right. Its theme is the conflict of good and evil. It is an expression of the fear of the dark, an examination of the nature and purpose of heroism, and the great statement of the Anglo-Saxon outlook and imagination.

The date of its composition was probably some time in the eighth century A.D., about 300 years after the settlement in Britain (as a consequence of the Roman withdrawal) of those Germanic tribes who were the ancestors of the Anglo-Saxons. It would be a mistake to suppose that Anglo-Saxon society of the eighth century was primitive and uncultured. On the contrary, it was a Christian, organized, and aristocratic civilization, one of whose kings, Offa of Mercia, was in a position to treat on equal terms with the great Charlemagne. An idea of the wealth and magnificence of an even earlier Anglo-Saxon society can be gleaned from a visit to the remarkable treasures, now exhibited in the British Museum, which were excavated from the Sutton Hoo burial ship.* Anglo-Saxon monasteries were seats of learning, whose libraries were filled with secular as well as religious literature. If the poet of *Beowulf* never read the *Aeneid* (and it is on the cards that he did), yet he is likely to have had access to it. *Beowulf*, in fact, is the product of a sophisticated culture.

At this point it may be convenient to set down a brief summary of the plot of the poem. *Beowulf* opens with an account of the funeral of Scyld, the mythical founder of the Danish Royal House. Scyld's descendant, Hrothgar, builds the great hall of Heorot. But a fiendish, half-human monster called Grendel, who lives in the fens, is angered by the sound of rejoicing in Heorot and attacks the hall by night, killing thirty of the Danes. He repeats his exploit and continues to ravage Heorot for twelve years, since neither Hrothgar nor his men are able to put an end to his depredations. News of this reaches the ears of Beowulf, a nephew of Hygelac, king of the Geats (a tribe living in Sweden). Beowulf decides to go to Hrothgar's assistance. With fourteen adventurers he sails to Denmark, and is received by Hrothgar in Heorot. After a banquet Beowulf and his Geats remain in the hall to wait for Grendel. When night has fallen the monster visits Heorot, bursts the door in, and kills and devours one of the Geats. But when he takes hold of Beowulf the hero seizes him and, after a terrible battle, wrenches off his arm. Grendel is mortally wounded and escapes to his lair. Next day a great feast is prepared in Heorot, at which Hrothgar and his queen Wealhtheow shower gifts on Beowulf and his men, while one of the court poets recites the song of Finn. But, following the banquet, when the Danes are asleep, Grendel's mother raids the hall and carries off one of Hrothgar's best-loved counsellors in revenge for her son's death. In the morning the Danes and Geats track her to the lake in whose depths she lives; Beowulf plunges in and kills

* For the bearing of these on the study of *Beowulf*, see Appendix: 'Sutton Hoo and *Beowulf*'.

her after an underwater duel at the lake-bottom. He cuts the head from Grendel's corpse, which he finds there, and returns with it to Heorot. Again there is a banquet, during which Hrothgar delivers a long moralizing speech of advice to the hero. The following day Beowulf and the Geats, laden with gifts, sail for home. When they reach the court of Hygelac they are banqueted, and, having told the story of his adventures, Beowulf presents his king with the treasures that Hrothgar has given him, in return receiving liberal gifts. This ends the first part of the poem.

After the death of Hygelac and of his son Heardred in the wars with the Franks and Swedes, Beowulf becomes king of the Geats and rules over them for fifty years. But towards the end of his reign his country is devastated by a Dragon, the sentinel of an ancient treasure which has been looted by a runaway slave, thus provoking its terrible guardian. The old hero decides to fight the Dragon single-handed, and having armed himself with an iron shield for protection against its flaming breath, sets out with eleven followers, including his kinsman Wiglaf. Before the battle commences the old king makes a long speech in which he recalls his youth, and especially the Geat feud with the Swedes. Taking leave of his companions, he challenges the Dragon, but his sword breaks during the fight and he finds himself overwhelmed by the Dragon's fiery exhalation. Terrified, all his friends run away except Wiglaf, who comes to his rescue. Together they kill the Dragon; but Beowulf has been mortally wounded and dies in the arms of Wiglaf. Filled with sorrow and anger, Wiglaf rebukes the runaways, and sends a messenger to the Geats to announce the king's death. In his speech the messenger foretells the disasters that will follow the death of Beowulf, recalling their former wars with the Franks and Swedes and prophesying that they will take their revenge now that the hero is no longer there to protect his people. The Geats then visit the scene of the fight. They carry away the treasure-hoard and push the corpse of the Dragon over a cliff into the sea. A funeral pyre is built, on which Beowulf's body is burnt. Over his remains the Geats build a huge mound, in which the Dragon's treasure is also placed. Twelve warriors ride round the barrow lamenting Beowulf and praising his virtues.

At first it seems rather naïve and unsophisticated, all this about lumbering monsters and fire-spewing dragons; and perhaps a bit crude and lacking in cohesion, for there appear to be two quite different tales, one about the Danes in Heorot worried by man-eating giants, and another concerning the Geats and their Dragon, linked together by the simple scheme of having the same hero for both stories. Indeed, the early critics and commentators of *Beowulf*, and a good many of the later ones, have been very sarcastic about the clumsiness of the plot. For the poem is a bit of a rag-bag as well, stuffed with fragments from the history of Scandinavian tribes, and spilling over with untidy-looking references to apparently irrelevant events and legends. But Professor J. R. R. Tolkien, in his famous essay, *Beowulf: The Monsters and the Critics*, was one of the first to show that the construction of the poem was rather more subtle than had been thought. He pointed out that it depended, like the alliterative measure in which the poem is written, on a balance – thesis and antithesis – rather than straightforward narrative. Thus the poem begins, and ends, with a funeral; and the first part, which tells of the hero's youth, is in contrast to the second, which deals with his old age. And if its story is concerned with monsters and dragons, it is not because the poet and his Anglo-Saxon audience were childishly fascinated by such phenomena, although they were aware of the possibility of their existence. For Beowulf, though a hero and a superman, is a human being. 'He is a man, and that for him and many is sufficient tragedy.'* The creatures against which he fights – the almost human Grendel and his mother, and later the primeval, more elemental Dragon – have symbolic value. Beowulf is on the side of the gods, but in the Northern mythology (which in spite of the Christianity that interpenetrates the poem, is its background) the gods, though on the right side, are not on the winning side. As W. P. Ker wrote: 'The winning side is Chaos and Unreason, but the gods, who are defeated, think that defeat no refutation.'† When in *Beowulf* the hero, after overcoming such nearly human opponents as Grendel (supposed to be descended from Cain, the

* J. R. R. Tolkien, *Beowulf: The Monsters and the Critics*, p. 260.
† W. P. Ker, *The Dark Ages*. London, 1904, p. 58.

first murderer), finally succumbs to a darker, older, primordial, and non-human antagonist, the Dragon, and we are given to understand that as a consequence of his deaths wars and calamities must inevitably destroy the people he tried to protect, the inference is a tragic but not a merely pessimistic one.

To return to the structure of *Beowulf*: one of its characteristics is the extraordinary number of episodes and digressions that are contained in it. Many of these considerably puzzled the early students of the poem, who invented a number of ingenious but unsatisfactory theories to account for them, theories which usually postulated either a composite authorship for the work or the existence of one or more interpolators. It is now generally agreed – and indeed obvious – that *Beowulf* is the work of a single poet, and that this poet was a Christian. * In a brilliant essay, *The Digressions in Beowulf*, M. Adrien Bonjour has discussed the artistic relevance of these episodes and asides. He concluded that the poet of *Beowulf* knew what he was about: everything that he put into his poem is there to add something to the effect of the whole. Far from being a rambling, incoherent affair, the poem is built up of themes, motifs, contrasts, and parallels, and is in fact as sophisticated in its construction and use of allusion as *The Waste Land* of T. S. Eliot. One example is the funeral of Scyld Scefing, with which the poem opens, foreshadowing Beowulf's obsequies at the end. Another may be found when Beowulf's defeat of Grendel is celebrated by one of Hrothgar's men in a song of praise, and the singer compares the hero with the mythical Sigemund who won fame by killing a dragon: thus bringing to Beowulf's first exploit an echo

---

* It used to be argued that *Beowulf* was a pagan poem, and that the 'Christian passages' in it were interpolations. But, as Miss Dorothy Whitelock has pointed out, the 'Christian element' not only permeates the poem but pervades even its language and imagery. The many allusions to Biblical events not only demonstrate that the poet was familiar with the scriptures, but that he could assume a similar familiarity on the part of his audience. At the same time, it should be remembered that the conversion of the Anglo-Saxons to Christianity was a comparatively recent event. The pagan ship-burial at Sutton Hoo took place only a century or so before the putative date of the composition of the poem. See *The Audience of Beowulf*, by Dorothy Whitelock. (Oxford, 1951.)

of his last. And so on. But to a modern audience some of the episodes and allusions are obscure because they depend for their understanding on a knowledge of the history of Scandinavian dynasties, a knowledge which the poet of *Beowulf* was able to assume on the part of the audience he was addressing. For instance, the eventual burning of Hrothgar's hall, and the usurpation of the Danish throne by his nephew Hrothulf, are more than once alluded to in the poem, though these events lie outside the actual scope of its story. The implications of such references were not lost on the Anglo-Saxon audience. They did not miss the ironic and sinister overtones of the incident at the banquet celebrating the defeat of Grendel, when Wealhtheow, Hrothgar's wife, commends her sons to the generosity of her husband's nephew Hrothulf. For this was the man who, as we know from other sources, was destined to wade in her children's blood to the Danish throne. And earlier, at the same banquet, Hrothgar's court poet sings a song about Finn, which at first appears to have nothing to do with the main theme of the poem. Yet it affords another of the grim and ironically-hinted analogues of which the *Beowulf* poet was so fond. For an old blood-feud was at that moment smouldering between Hrothgar's people and another tribe, the Heathobards; and, as we learn later on in the poem itself, at the time of the banquet Hrothgar was engaged in trying to settle this feud by marrying his own daughter Freawaru to Ingeld, the leader of the Heathobards. And what is the song of Finn about? It tells of a blood-feud, in which a queen is torn between opposing loyalties owed to her husband and to her brother, who fought on different sides; of the official settling of this feud, which was yet so ineradicable that it burst out again, disastrously. Thus the song of Finn from one point of view suggests a left-handed prefiguring of the luckless result of Hrothgar's attempt to settle the Danish–Heathobard feud, and of the dilemma in which his own daughter Freawaru, divided in loyalty between her husband and her father, was to find herself.

In this way the *Beowulf* poet builds up an atmosphere of doom, which Beowulf's victories over Grendel and Grendel's mother scarcely dispel. It is a human evil – the Heathobard feud – and not the monsters, which in the end destroy Hrothgar's palace. This effect is paralleled in the second part of the poem, which deals with the Dragon fight, in the reminders of the quarrels of Beowulf's own people, the Geats, with the Franks and Swedes, and in the indications that after the death of Beowulf there will be little to prevent the enemies of the Geats from annihilating them. In a sense Grendel and his mother are a manifestation of the evil that will overtake the Danes, and the Dragon of the disaster which is to destroy the Geats. Many minor touches go to the creation of this aura of overhanging catastrophe. To take one instance, the poet interrupts his description of Beowulf's fight with the Dragon to give a long and apparently irrelevant account of the history of the sword with which his kinsman Wiglaf comes to the hero's rescue. But the point about the sword is that it was a trophy taken in battle from the brother of the Swedish king by Wiglaf's father: and it is thus a reminder of an unsettled blood-feud, and can therefore furnish the Swedes with an excuse to declare war when Wiglaf inherits the Geat throne after Beowulf's death.

Another effect of what are called 'the historical elements' in *Beowulf* – the subsidiary stories of the Danes and the Geats – is to give the poem greater depth and verisimilitude. Hrothgar, the Danish king, is a 'historical' character, and the site of his palace of Heorot has been identified with the village of Leire on the island of Seeland in Denmark. The Geat king Hygelac really existed, and his unlucky expedition against the Franks, referred to several times in the poem, is mentioned by Gregory of Tours in the *Historia Francorum* and has been given the approximate date of A.D. 521.* We must remember that to Anglo-Saxons of the eighth century the main events of the wars and feuds of the Danes, Swedes, and Geats of the sixth century were probably quite as familiar as those of the Napoleonic wars are to a modern reader. Beowulf, Grendel, and the Dragon clearly belong to the 'mythical elements' – though it is worth noting that these distinctions might have appeared unimportant to the audience of *Beowulf*. But the main relevance of the subsidiary stories of the feuds between the Danes and the Heathobards, and between the Geats and the Swedes and the Franks, to the whole poem, lies in the ironic effect

* See Note 15 at the end of the book.

which the poet extracts from them so often and unfailingly. After describing how Hrothgar built Heorot, 'the greatest banqueting hall ever known', and picturing its magnificence and the feast held to celebrate its completion, the poet immediately reminds us: 'Yet it was to endure leaping flames, when in the course of time a deadly feud between Hrothgar and his son-in-law should be kindled by an act of vengeance.' It is at this significant point that Grendel is introduced: the outcast monster who, angered by the song of Creation whch is sung in Heorot, begins to ravage the hall. And generally it may be said that the poet uses the subsidiary 'historical' stories to hammer home the temporal nature of Beowulf's heroic achievements. There is irony latent in the fact that although Beowulf purges Heorot and kills the Dragon, the Danes and the Geats whom he tries to help are destined to be destroyed by the consequences of their own deeds.

The idea of the transitoriness and impermanence of the material world is a favourite theme of much Old English literature. One of the most famous images in Bede's *Ecclesiastical History* (composed in Latin, but one of the first works to be translated into Old English) is that which compares a man's life to a sparrow flying from the winter darkness into a lighted hall, into the warmth and cheerfulness for a moment, then out once more into the night. This acute awareness that everything must come to an end, all splendour perish, and all power disappear – 'lif is læne, eal scæceth, leoht ond lif somod' (life is ephemeral, everything vanishes, light and life together) – is characteristic of the Anglo-Saxon imagination. Perhaps those reminders of a past and mysterious splendour with which Britain was then filled – the derelict towns, crumbling villas, and ruined forts that had been left behind by Roman civilization – lay at the root of this obsession, no less than the pagan and Germanic antecedents of the Anglo-Saxons. *Beowulf* is a Christian poem with a more or less pagan hero. The consolation of Beowulf is not a Christian consolation but a heroic one; and, as Professor Tolkien has said, perhaps this consolation is the more moving because it is given by a Christian poet looking back at a pagan and heroic past that was still recent.

For what is the consolation of Beowulf? It is the theme of the poem – *lof* – a more or less untranslatable word which means roughly the praise and esteem of one's contemporaries. This theme is stated at the beginning of the work:

> *Lof-dædum sceal*
> in mægþa gehwæm   man geþeon

For among all peoples it is only through *those actions which merit praise* that a man may prosper.

and it finds its echo in Beowulf's epitaph, in the last two lines of the poem:

> manna mildust   ond mon-þwærust,
> leodum liðost   ond *lof-geornost*.

The gentlest and most gracious of men, the kindest to his people and the *most desirous of renown*.

The idea is that fame is the most precious thing that a man can have because it is about all that survives in a very transient world. Thus Beowulf consoles Hrothgar for the death of his favourite counsellor:

It is better for a man to avenge his friend than to mourn him long. We must all expect an end to life in this world; let him who can win fame before death, because that is a dead man's best memorial.

The pagan temper was tough and fatalistic. *Wyrd gæþ swa hit sceal* (Fate must decide) says Beowulf before he fights Grendel. *Wyrd* – another key-word, almost as difficult to translate as *lof* – means 'fate', 'fortune', 'what comes to pass'. Relating the story of a narrow escape from death, Beowulf comments:

> Wyrd oft nereð
> unfægne eorl,   þonne his ellen deah.

Unless he is already doomed, fortune (*wyrd*) is apt to favour the man who keeps his nerve.

Although the poet of *Beowulf* was a Christian speaking to a Christian audience, the background of pagan philosophy breaks through the newer ethos in such remarks, which appear to confuse fate with God. In such passages it seems that the Christian concept of the Almighty had not been completely superimposed upon the pagan idea of *wyrd*. But that it was superimposed the poet makes

:lear in the passage that describes how Beowulf was nearly killed by Grendel's mother, yet managed to defeat her in the end:

For God brought about the victory. Once Beowulf had struggled to his feet, the holy and omniscient ruler of the sky easily settled the issue in favour of the right.

Once Beowulf had struggled to his feet. God helps those who help themselves: the human being is not without responsibility. 'Fortune is apt to favour the man who keeps his nerve.'

And when Beowulf dies, the poet comments:

The soul left his body to seek the reward of the just.

But Beowulf is not presented as either a specifically Christian or specifically pagan hero. One of the remarkable things about the poem is the historical tact displayed by the poet in addressing to a Christian audience a work which is set, in time, in a pagan world. The poet of *Beowulf* avoids the open and disconcerting anachronisms which one finds in comparable works – the *Nibelungenlied*, for example. There are references to the Old Testament in *Beowulf* – for instance the mention of Cain and Abel and of the story of the Flood – but there is no allusion to Christ or the New Testament. This must have been deliberate: for, of course, the Old Testament does not jar with, or inhibit, the heroic temper in the same way as the New Testament with its doctrine of the redemption and forgiveness of sins.

Rather, Beowulf is a type of ideal hero and ideal king. He is constantly compared with Heremod, a Danish king who was an example of the worst kind of leader. Heremod was cruel, parsimonious, and took the lives of his own retainers. But kings were supposed to be the guardians of their people: they were expected to look after the booty that they and their followers had won, and to share it generously and equitably. The great virtue in a society such as this was loyalty: therefore the worst crime was treachery. The code of the blood-feud was paramount. This code demanded for the death of a man the vengeance of his kinsmen and retainers: it was their moral and social obligation. Thus the most horrifying and unforgivable crime, because impossible to avenge, was the murder of a blood-relation. And in the same way the worst and most dishonourable thing a man could do was to desert his leader in battle, or to become a follower of the man who slew him. The dying Beowulf could claim that he had fulfilled his duties as a king and upheld the heroic code:

I have reigned over this people for half a century, and there was not a king of any neighbouring nation who dared to attack me with an army or to threaten me with war. The destiny allotted to me on earth I endured; what was mine I defended well. Though wounded to death, I can rejoice in all these things; because when the life quits my body God cannot accuse me of the murder of my kin.

The poem of *Beowulf* presents a clear picture of a heroic age and society.

But this is not its real claim on our attention. *Beowulf*, as I have already said, is not merely a historical document, but a great poem in its own right. For its theme has the weight of great poetry. It is about how the human being ought to behave when he is without hope. It affirms the human being in a world where everything is transient, whether life, happiness, power, or splendour; where darkness too quickly follows upon light, just as the long northern winter overwhelms the brief season of spring. It ends with the smoke of a funeral fire: the primeval Dragon defeated, but the man lying dead, with disaster waiting round the corner for the people he defended. But his glory survives; and that is the consolation. It is one that has been re-expressed in our own time by a great contemporary poet:

There is only the fight to recover what has been lost
And found and lost again and again: and now, under conditions
That seem unpropitious. But perhaps neither gain nor loss.
For us, there is only the trying. The rest is not our business.

A NOTE ON THE TRANSLATION

My aim in translating the poem of *Beowulf* has been to produce, if I could, a readable version in contemporary English prose and to bring out those qualities of the original which in other translations, it seems to me, have been either overlooked or overlaid.

Although *Beowulf* has been not inappropriately described as an elegiac poem and is only a little over 3,000 lines in length, it is really a primary epic – that is to say, one that depends for its material on oral rather than written sources, and is meant to be recited rather than read. Now one of the principal *poetic* attributes of primary epics lies in their construction, narrative interest, and presentation of story. The *Iliad* and the *Odyssey* are examples; the *Aeneid* and *Paradise Lost* are not. The latter are secondary or *literary* epics, and their poetic effect depends less on the story than upon the individuality as well as the magnificence of their style and diction. It can be maintained, I think, that *how* the *Iliad* is presented (i.e. its plot and construction) is at least as important to its total poetic impact as the way in which it is composed (i.e. its individuality of style and diction). But in the case of the *Aeneid* (or of *Paradise Lost*) the poetic impact is much more dependent upon individuality of style and diction than upon plot or construction. Coleridge once asked, 'If you take from Virgil his diction and metre, what do you leave him?' Thus, confronted with an *Aeneid* or a *Paradise Lost*, a translator who wants to do a satisfactory job must replace their quality of style and diction with an effective substitute – which is to say that he must be a poet himself, and translate their poetry into something better than prose or verse – into his own poetry in fact, as Dryden did when he translated Virgil. Or to put it in another way, and very roughly, in the *Aeneid* and *Paradise Lost* the story is a peg on which the poet hangs his poem, while in Homer and *Beowulf* the poem is the story, and vice versa. Therefore to render the *Iliad*, the *Odyssey*, or *Beowulf* into prose is not only feasible but in some ways more desirable than to translate them into verse. Verse which is not poetry obscures the story, and therefore the poem, without providing an adequate substitute for the style of the original.

Anyone who translates a work that has been rendered into English as often as *Beowulf* owes much to his predecessors, if only because he is more easily able to see and avoid mistakes and pitfalls. To my mind the principal error made by earlier translators has been their effort to find an equivalent for the archaic poetic diction which characterizes Anglo-Saxon poetry and especially *Beowulf*. They have had very good reasons (which I shall indicate later) for trying to do so, but I believe that, judging from results, more is lost than won in the attempt. The Anglo-Saxon verse in which *Beowulf* is written has its own diction, distinct from prose, almost amounting to a language within a language. Generally speaking, Old English prose is lucid and straightforward; but Old English verse is quite another kettle of fish. It uses archaic and poetic terms which are not employed in prose, as well as compounds (known as 'kennings') that have to be deciphered like riddles or the clues of a crossword puzzle. (Those who complain of the teasing obscurity of modern English verse might reflect how much knottier Old English poetry was.) For instance, a simple statement like 'A ship sailed over the sea' might in Anglo-Saxon verse be put in this way: 'The foamy-neck came over the gannet's-bath', or 'The twisted-prow sailed over the whale's-road'. There are also any number of compound words. 'Soldier' can be expressed in dozens of ways – 'shield-bearer', 'battle-hero', 'spear-fighter', and many more. The descriptive compounds for 'king' are nearly as plentiful: 'war-chief', 'gold-friend', 'treasure-guardian', in addition to allusive phrases like 'protector of the people', 'shield of the fighting-men', and so on. This vocabulary and habit of diction constitute the special beauty, richness, and intricacy of Anglo-Saxon poetry, which is as glittering and mazy, yet formal, as, say, the design on the golden belt-buckle recovered from the Sutton Hoo burial-ship. And it constitutes the principal difficulty of translating any Anglo-Saxon poem satisfactorily. Ezra Pound brought it off in his remarkable and famous version of *The Seafarer*, which cannot be too strongly recommended to anyone who wants to get the real 'feel' of Old English poetry. On the other hand, Charles Scott-Moncrieff's verse translation of *Beowulf*, which attempts an absolutely literal rendering, even to an imitation of the original 'kennings' and alliterative measure, remains, finally, a monument of unreadable ingenuity – indeed, it is hardly unfair to say that a knowledge of Anglo-Saxon is necessary to elucidate it. And among the prose translations of *Beowulf*, the best and most accurate, by John R. Clark-Hall (revised in 1950 by Professor C. L. Wrenn), also tries to reproduce the archaic flavour and kenning phraseology of the original. But the result is a queer jargon:

The whole band rose, the grey-haired patriarch-Scylding would fain go to his bed. Exceeding much did the Geat, the brave shield-warrior, desire to rest. Straightway the chamberlain, who in courtesy looked after all a noble's needs – such needs as that day warrior travellers used to have – guided him forth, weary with his adventure, come from far. Then the noble-hearted man reposed; the chamber towered aloft, spacious and gold-adorned; the stranger slept within, until the swarthy raven, blithe of heart, harbingered the radiance of heaven.

Yet it is impossible not to be sensible of the cogent arguments that Professor Tolkien, in his notable preface to the latest revision of Clark-Hall's translation, puts forward against attempts to render the artificial, archaic, and poetic diction of *Beowulf* into straightforward and contemporary English prose. So much is lost by a plain translation that the reader obtains no real idea of the complexity, verbal build-up, and effectiveness of the poem in the original, nor of the overtones which are so often present. On the other hand, to try to indicate the poetic, archaic, and literary diction of *Beowulf* by using such 'poetic' and 'literary' words as 'fain' and 'blithe' – which are in fact not literary, poetic, or archaic, but the bankrupt currency of nineteenth-century romantic verse – strips the work of its force and dignity, without capturing the tone of the Anglo-Saxon poem; and, which is just as bad a crime, may mislead readers into supposing that there is fustian in the original.

To translate *Beowulf* into Wardour Street English seems to me, therefore, a mistake; yet it would be equally wrong to render the poem in colloquial prose. There remains a middle style. The argument against the middle style is that in comparison with the original it seems colourless. With this I do not entirely agree: in any case, better no colours than faked ones. When the leaves are off a great oak it is still possible to admire the nobility and spread of its branches. It is not necessary to trick them out with imitation foliage.

As I have said, one of the poetic virtues of a primary epic is to be found in its construction, plot, and narrative interest. Therefore, in my version, I have aimed at revealing these qualities in the poem of *Beowulf*. This has also meant bearing in mind the fact that I was translating, not merely from one language into another, but from one medium into another; that is, from poetry into prose. Where the Anglo-Saxon poet has written 'swan's way' and the meaning is 'sea', I have not used the evocative and poetic paraphrase. On the same principle I have used the terms 'Geat' and 'Dane' throughout, instead of translating the other connotations employed by the poet – 'Storm-Geats', 'Ring-Danes', and so on. Often I have simply given Beowulf's name instead of translating the formulas 'son of Ecgtheow' or 'kinsman of Hygelac' where these seemed uneuphonic, cumbrous, or unnecessarily long-winded. Occasionally, though very seldom, I have incorporated a gloss: e.g. the phrase 'ecghete aþumswerian' (lit. 'blade-hate of sons-in-law and fathers-in-law') I have rendered thus: 'a deadly feud between Hrothgar and his son-in-law' – a clarification of the implications of the text. While my main endeavour has been to produce a readable prose translation of the poem rather than a word-for-word version of the text, I have been at pains to make it as exact and correct as possible. My translation is based on the editions of Klaeber and Wrenn, whose interpretations of the text and of its many crucial passages I have in general followed (but see Notes at the end of the book). But my version is not offered as a mere crib for reading the poem in the original Anglo-Saxon. That purpose has been answered by Clark-Hall. It has been my aim not to distract the reader's attention from the story that is presented

NOTE ON THE TRANSLATION

by the poet of *Beowulf* by attempting to recreate his allusive use of language. The Anglo-Saxon *scop* was able to employ a highly formalized and artificial diction because his audience was trained and accustomed to that kind of idiom. But his translator must remember that he is a writer of contemporary English prose competing with other writers of contemporary English prose for the attention of his readers.

September 1956

DAVID WRIGHT

A NOTE ON PUNCTUATION

The punctuation of the MS of the poem is limited and not consistent (at least it does not appear to be so in the light of present knowledge of punctuation in Old English MSS, which may represent advice to reciters as well as to readers). Therefore my punctuation is modern, though based on that supplied by Wrenn and Klaeber in their editions. But I have retained the numbers marking the separate sections of the poem, as given in the original MS of *Beowulf*. Sections 29 and 30 are not numbered. This confusion may be the result either of incorrect numbering in an earlier MS or of the fact that the second scribe of the present MS had begun work just before this point.

BEOWULF

Hear! We know of the bygone glory of the Danish kings, and the heroic exploits of those princes. Scyld Scefing, in the face of hostile armies, used often to bring nations into subjection, and strike terror in the hearts of their leaders. In the beginning he had been picked up as a castaway; but he afterwards found consolation for this misfortune. For his power and fame increased until each of his overseas neighbours was forced to submit and pay him tribute. He was an excellent king.

Later a son was born to him in his stronghold, a young prince whom God, seeing the misery which the Danes had so long endured when they were kingless, sent to be their comfort. The Almighty granted him renown. Beowulf, son of Scyld,[1] became famous in Denmark, and his fame spread everywhere. Thus, while still under his father's protection, a young prince should by his goodness and generous gifts so manage affairs that later on his companions may give him support and his people their loyalty in time of war. For among all peoples it is only through those actions which merit praise that a man may prosper.

Scyld's hour came when he was in the prime of his strength. After a long reign the king departed into the care of God. His dearest retainers carried the beloved Danish leader to the sea's edge, as he had commanded while he could yet speak. Rime-crusted and ready to sail, a royal vessel with curved prow lay in harbour. They set down their dear king amidships, close by the mast. A mass of treasure was brought there from distant parts. No ship, they say, was ever so well equipped with swords, corselets, weapons,

and armour. On the king's breast rested a heap of jewels
which were to go with him far out into the keeping of the
sea. The Danes furnished Scyld Scefing with offerings from
their treasury that were as good as the gifts provided by
those who, when he was a child, launched him alone across
the ocean. High overhead they set his golden standard;
then, surrendering him to the sea, they sadly allowed it to
bear him off. And no one, whether a counsellor in hall or a
soldier in the field, can truly say who received that cargo.[2]

I

AFTER his father's death Beowulf king of the Danes gov-
erned his stronghold and was for a long time famous among
nations. Then the great Healfdene was born. Healfdene, a
fierce old veteran, ruled the Danes all his life. To him four
children in all were born – Heorogar, Hrothgar, Halga the
Good, and a daughter who, we are told, became the con-
sort of Onela, the Swedish king.

Such success in arms and so great a fame attended Hroth-
gar that his kinsmen were eager to serve under him, and in
this way the number of his young retainers increased until
he had a formidable army. It came into his mind to com-
mand the erection of a building that should be the greatest
banqueting hall ever known, in which he could apportion
to young and old everything that God had entrusted to
him, with the exception of public lands and human life. So,
as I have heard, orders were dispatched all over the world
for its furbishing; and in a short time the enormous build-
ing was completed. The king called it Heorot, and kept his
promise at the feast, when he distributed rings and treasure.
Tall and wide-gabled, the hall towered overhead; yet it was

to endure terrible and leaping flames, when in the course of time a deadly feud between Hrothgar and his son-in-law should be kindled by an act of violence.

At that time a mighty fiend who lived in darkness suffered greatly. Their happiness, which he heard daily resounding from the hall, grated on his ear: the harp-music, and clear song of a poet relating the creation of man from the earliest times – how God made the world, a shining plain encircled by the sea, and through His power established the sun and moon to light its inhabitants; how He decked the face of the earth with leaves and branches, and besides gave life to all that moves. In this way the fighting-men were happily living, until the fiend from hell began to work them mischief.

The grim demon was called Grendel, a notorious ranger of the borderlands, who inhabited the fastnesses of moors and fens. This unhappy being had long lived in the land of monsters, because God had damned him along with the children of Cain. For the eternal Lord avenged the killing of Abel. He took no delight in that feud, but banished Cain from humanity because of his crime. From Cain were hatched all evil progenies: ogres, hobgoblins, and monsters, not to mention the giants who fought so long against God – for which they suffered due retribution.

2

AT nightfall Grendel set out to visit the great hall to see how the Danes had settled down in it after they had finished drinking. He found a band of soldiers sleeping after a banquet, dead to care and human misery. Savage, exasperated, the grim and greedy demon was ready in a trice. He pounced on thirty men where they slept. Then, glutted with slaughter, he went home to his lair exulting over his spoil.

By daybreak the ferocity of Grendel was clear to everyone. A great cry went up in the morning; lamentation followed the revels. The famous king felt keenly for his retainers when the tracks of the fiend were discovered, and fell prey to grief. The struggle was too harsh, evil, and unremitting. For there was no respite, but the next night Grendel, without the least scruple (he was too much bent on such things), committed further mischief and murder. Soon it was easy enough to find a man who looked for sleeping-quarters farther off, or for a bed in the outbuildings, once the glaring evidence of the enmity of Heorot's latest henchman [3] became manifest. Whoever escaped from the fiend took care to keep out of harm's way afterwards.

In this way Grendel held the upper hand and fought against right, alone against everyone, until the great hall stood derelict. This went on for a long time. For twelve years the king of the Danes suffered all kinds of misery and distress. Sorrowful ballads spread to all quarters the news that Grendel was on the war-path, waging year after year a murderous and interminable feud with Hrothgar. He would make no peace with any of the Danish host, nor would he be bought off. Neither could any of the counsellors expect lavish compensation at the hands of the killer.[4] But the demon, a black shadow of death, prowled, lay in ambush, and plotted against young and old. Night after night he patrolled the fog-bound moors. Who can say where such demons may range in their wanderings?

Thus the malign outcast, like the enemy of man that he was, made frequent attacks and produced unspeakable havoc. In the darkness of night he occupied the rich hall of Heorot; but he could not approach the treasure-throne because of the Lord, nor could Grendel know His love.[5] This affliction broke the spirit of the Danish king. Many leading Danes held councils to devise some plan to discover the best and boldest course to take against this reign of terror. Sometimes they promised sacrifices to the heathen shrines, praying to the Devil for help against the oppression which afflicted them all. Such was their practice – and such the hope of a heathen people. Hell was in their hearts; they knew nothing of a Creator, the true God, judge of all acts; nor did they know how to worship the glorious king of heaven. Woe to him whose perversity shall thrust his soul into the abyss of fire, with no hope of change or of consolation. But well for him who can stand before God after death, and invoke the protection of his Father's arms.

3

IN this way Hrothgar perpetually brooded over his present trouble. Even that wise prince was unable to ward off the affliction, because the feud in which his people were involved was so cruel, harsh, and long drawn out. It was a stinging trial and the worst of the horrors of darkness.

But one of Hygelac's followers, in his far-off country, heard about Grendel's doings. Well-born, stalwart, and the strongest of living men, this man was a hero among the Geats. He ordered a seaworthy vessel to be equipped, and announced that he was crossing the sea to pay a visit to Hrothgar, since that famous prince stood in need of men. The wise did not really blame him for undertaking this expedition, although they loved him; but they urged him on, and watched the omens. From among the Geats the hero picked the bravest men that he could find, and took fourteen of them with him to the ship. Himself an experienced seaman, he led the way to the shore.

Soon the boat was launched and afloat below the head-land. The soldiers, in full harness, came aboard by the prow and stowed a cargo of polished armour and magnificent war-equipment amidships, while the sea churned and surf beat against the beach. Then the adventurers, bound on the voyage they had eagerly desired, pushed off their well-braced vessel. With a fair wind behind and a bone in her teeth, the curved prow skimmed over the sea like a bird, until in due course on the second day she had sailed far enough for the voyagers to make a landfall – glistening cliffs, high mountains, and broad promontories. With clanging armour the Geats quickly leapt ashore, made fast the ship, and gave thanks to God for an easy passage.

From a rampart the Danish coastguard who had to watch the sea approaches saw them carrying over the gang-way their glittering shields and battle equipment, till his mind was on fire to discover who these men might be. Hrothgar's officer therefore rode down to the beach, vehemently brandishing the great spear which he held, and challenged:

'What sort of people may you be who have come in arms from across the ocean in that great ship? For years I have been coastguard, and kept watch over the sea so that no pirate fleet might raid the Danish coast. No armed men have ever ventured to land here so openly! Nor did you make certain of either the permission or consent of our leaders. But I have never anywhere seen a more formidable champion than that armed man in your midst, who is cer-tainly no mere retainer carrying weapons, unless his heroic bearing and appearance belie him. Yet in case you are spies I must know all about you before you go further into Danish territory. Now listen to plain speaking, you foreign seamen. You had better tell me why you have come, and at once.'

4

THE leader of the band began to speak. 'We are Geats by race, and eat at the table of Hygelac. My father was a famous chieftain; his name was Ecgtheow. The old man lived to a ripe old age before he died, and is remembered by wise men throughout the world. We have come to pay a friendly visit to your king, Hrothgar son of Healfdene. Give us good advice, because we are on an important errand to the lord of the Danes, and one which I suppose is not likely to remain secret. You will know – if what we have heard is true – that there is some sort of evildoer among the Danes, a hidden enemy who at dead of night and in brutal fashion inflicts incalculable harm, disgrace, and havoc. In all sincerity I think I can advise the worthy prince Hrothgar how to overthrow the fiend – that is, if his afflictions are destined ever to end, his troubles to subside, and better times to return to him. Otherwise he must put up with tribulation so long as his great hall stands upon its eminence.'

From horseback the coastguard, a resolute officer, answered: 'A good soldier who has his wits about him must know how to distinguish between promise and performance. I understand that this is a troop friendly to the Danish king. Pass, carrying arms and equipment, and I will be your guide. In the meantime I shall appoint my officers to protect your ship against pirates. This will be a guard of honour for your newly-tarred vessel as it lies on the beach, until the time comes for its snaky prow to carry over the seas back to the country of the Geats a very popular man – to such a hero it will be given to come safely through the encounter.'

Upon this they got ready to go. The great ship, moored, rode quietly at anchor. Above their helmets glittered boar-crests of tempered gold keeping watch over the Geats, whose hearts were filled with excitement. The company marched in quick step until they caught sight of a handsome timbered hall, embellished with gold, the seat of Hrothgar and the most celebrated building in the world, whose splendour blazed abroad over many lands. The coastguard pointed out that glistening home of heroes to them, so that they could march directly towards it. Turning his horse, he said: 'It is time for me to return; may the almighty Father through His grace keep you safe in your enterprise. I must go back to the sea to keep watch against hostile bands.'

5

THE road, paved with stone, served as a guide to the company. Each tough hand-linked coat of mail sparkled, and the shimmering ringlets of iron clinked in their corselets. When they arrived in armour at the hall, the sea-beaten men unslung their broad double-proofed shields and ranged them against the palace wall. Then they seated themselves on the bench; their corselets rang. The seafarers' weapons, iron-headed ash spears, were neatly piled. They were a well-equipped company.

While they waited, a distinguished-looking chieftain questioned the soldiers about their lineage. 'Whence have you brought these golden-plated shields, grey corselets and helmets, and that stack of spears? I am Hrothgar's attendant officer. But I have never seen a larger or a bolder company of newcomers; and I am sure it is out of daring and the spirit of adventure, not because of exile or banishment, that you have come to visit Hrothgar.'

Helmeted, the leader of the Geats answered him in firm tones: 'We are Hygelac's men; and my name is Beowulf. I shall explain my errand to Hrothgar, your illustrious king, if he will be good enough to grant us an audience.' To this Wulfgar (a Wendel prince, whose courage and acumen were famous) replied: 'I shall ask the lord of the Danes, our illustrious prince and giver of rings, concerning your expedition as you request, and inform you immediately of his answer.'

With this, Wulfgar turned quickly to where grey-haired old Hrothgar sat among his chieftains. The herald, well-versed in the custom of the court, advanced until he stood before the Danish king. Wulfgar addressed his lord: 'A party of Geats, whose leader is named Beowulf, has arrived from overseas. They beg audience of you, Sir. Do not refuse to speak with them, gracious Hrothgar! By their equipment they would seem to deserve respect, and the chieftain who led these soldiers here is without doubt a man of prowess.'

6

HROTHGAR replied: 'I knew him when he was a lad. His father was Ecgtheow, to whom Hrethel the Geat gave the hand of his only daughter; and now his son has confidently come to pay a visit to an old friend. Seamen who used to take my precious gifts to the Geats report that he has the strength of thirty men in the grip of his hand. I am sure that God has sent him to the help of the Danes against the terror of Grendel! I must offer the hero gifts for his daring. Make haste and invite them all to come in to meet my band of kinsmen – and say that they are welcome visitors to the Danish people.'

Wulfgar went to the door of the hall and delivered the message. 'I am commanded by the victorious king of the Danes to tell you that he knows your lineage, and that he welcomes such stout-hearted seafarers. You are permitted to enter Hrothgar's presence in armour, and wearing helmets, but leave your shields and javelins here to await the result of the parley.'

At this the chieftain and his followers rose to their feet: they made a fine body of men. Some remained behind to guard their weapons, in obedience to their leader's command. In quick step the Geats, led by their guide, marched under the rafters of Heorot. Helmeted, the hero advanced till he stood in the hall before the throne. Then in his glittering corselet of chainmail, the work of a dexterous smith, Beowulf spoke up.

'I salute you, Hrothgar! I am a nephew of Hygelac, and one of his followers. In my youth I have undertaken many notable exploits. I heard about the Grendel affair in my native country; for seamen relate that this great hall stands empty and useless to all once the sun sets below the horizon. So the best and wisest among my countrymen urged me to visit you, King Hrothgar, because they knew of my vast strength. They were eye-witnesses of it when, stained with the blood of my adversaries, I emerged from a fight in which I destroyed an entire family of giants – capturing five of them – besides killing, by night, a number of seamonsters. Although hard pressed, I destroyed the brutes (who had courted trouble) and avenged their attacks upon the Geats. And now I mean to deal single-handed with the monstrous Grendel. King of the Danes, protector of fighting-men, I shall ask of you one favour, which you will not deny to me now that I have come so far. It is that I alone, with my tough company of fighting-men, may be allowed to purge Heorot.

'They tell me that in his vainglory the monster is contemptuous of weapons. Therefore, as I wish to keep the good opinion of my lord Hygelac, I propose to dispense with any kind of sword or shield during the combat. Foe against foe, I shall fight the fiend to the death with my bare hands. Whichever of us is killed must resign himself to the verdict of God. Should Grendel prevail, as he has often done, I suppose that he will eat the Geat people, the flower of men, fearlessly in the hall of battle. And if death claims me, there will be no need for you to go to the expense of funeral rites, because Grendel will be in possession of my bloodstained corpse and will carry it off to devour. He will stain the swamps with my blood, and swallow me up without the least remorse; in which case you will have no need to trouble about the disposal of my body. If I am killed in combat, send to Hygelac the coat of mail which I am wearing. For it is the best corselet in the world, the work of Weland Smith, and an heirloom that once belonged to my grandfather Hrethel. Fate must decide.'

7

HROTHGAR, shield of the Danes, replied: 'My dear Beowulf, you have paid us this visit out of kindness to fight in our defence. Your father brought about such a ruinous feud when he killed Heatholaf of the Wilfings, that the Geats, for fear of a war, were unable to give him shelter. So he crossed the sea to visit the Danes. At the time I was a young man who had only recently begun to rule over the Danish people and govern this great kingdom with its wealthy stronghold. My elder brother Heorogar – a better man than myself – had just died. In time I settled the feud with money, sending many valuable old treasures overseas to the Wilfings, while your father gave me his parole.

'But it wrings my heart to tell anyone of the ravages and disgrace that the malice of Grendel has inflicted on Heorot. My retainers and my fighting-men have dwindled away. Their fate overtook them at the frightful onslaught of Grendel. Surely God can hold back that maniacal killer! Often and often, over their cups, a party of pot-valiant men has sworn to stay behind in Heorot to fight Grendel with their swords. But the next morning at daybreak this hall would be stained with carnage, the benches wet with blood, and I would have so many loyal followers the fewer, all of them dead. Now you must sit down to banquet; and when the time comes, express your thoughts and your confidence in victory to the men, just as you feel inspired.' [6]

A bench was cleared, so that the Geats could sit together in the banqueting hall. There, in the pride of their strength, those bold fighting-men took their seats. A servant who carried an ornamented ale-cup performed the office of pouring out the sparkling beer. From time to time a clear-voiced poet sang in Heorot. The soldiers, a large crowd of Danes and Geats, began to enjoy themselves.

8

UNFERTH, son of Ecglaf, who occupied a place of honour near the feet of the Danish king, spoke up. The enterprise of Beowulf greatly annoyed him, because he could not bear the thought that any living man might win more distinction than himself. So he broached a thorny topic:

'Are you the same Beowulf who competed with Breca, and raced against him in the open sea in that swimming

contest, when either out of conceit or foolhardiness the two
of you risked your lives upon the deep? There was nobody,
whether friend or foe, who could dissuade you from that
wretched exploit when you swam the sea. The pair of you
thrashed away with hands and arms through the scudding
wintry waves, and drudged in the water for a week. But
Breca was stronger. He beat you. One morning the sea cast
him up on the coast of Norway, and from there he made
his way home to his own country, where he had people,
treasure, and a fine stronghold to look after. He was the be-
loved king of the Brondings. Yet Breca son of Beanstan
faithfully kept his bargain with you. That is why, although
you have always been successful in battle, I expect a poor
showing if you dare to watch a whole night for Grendel at
close quarters.'

'What!' retorted Beowulf. 'Unferth, my friend, half-
seas over as you are, you have had a good deal to say about
Breca and his exploits! But I tell you for a fact that I am a
stronger swimmer than anybody else. When Breca and I
were young we made a bargain – we were boys at the time
– that we would chance our lives out at sea. This we did.
While swimming, each carried a naked sword in hand to
defend ourselves against whales. Breca could not swim far
from me because I was faster than he in the water; and I had
no intention of leaving him. We stayed together for five
nights until a storm drove us apart; a tempestuous sea, the
most bitter weather, nightfall, and the north wind, turned
savagely against us. The waves roughened, and the crea-
tures of the deep were lashed into fury. Then the golden
corselet that I wore, my tough hand-linked coat of mail,
helped me against my attackers. Some fearful monster took
fast hold of me and dragged me to the bottom; however, I
had the luck to get at the brute with the point of my sword,
and in the hurly-burly I dispatched it.

9

'In this manner my assailants pressed me hard and often. But I dealt with them in the right way with my stout sword. The killers did not have the pleasure of gorging themselves upon me for their dinner on the sea-floor. On the contrary, the next morning they were lying high and dry on the foreshore, riddled with wounds. My sword had made an end of them, and they were no longer to menace seamen voyaging on the high seas. And when the sun, the gleaming beacon of God, made its appearance in the east, the sea subsided so that I could catch sight of windswept cliffs and firths. For unless he is already doomed, fortune is apt to favour the man who keeps his nerve. However it was my luck to kill, sword in hand, nine sea-monsters. I cannot remember hearing of a harder battle by night anywhere in the world, or of anybody in worse danger at sea than I was.

'Yet, though almost at my last gasp, I escaped with my life from the monsters' clutches; and later the ocean currents carried me through heaving seas to Lapland. I have yet to hear of like encounters and exploits told about you. I will not now boast too much about this, but up to the present neither you nor Breca with your shining swords have performed so bold a feat of arms, though indeed you, Unferth, were the killer of your brothers: for which, clever as you are, you will certainly be damned in hell. Listen to me, Unferth! It is a fact that Grendel would never have done such damage to your king, nor wreaked such havoc in Heorot, if you had the fighting spirit with which you credit yourself. On the contrary, Grendel has discovered that he need not take very much notice of either the hostility or the onslaught of the victorious Danes, your countrymen. He takes toll of them and spares nobody, behaves just as he likes, kills, destroys, and snaps his fingers at the Danes! But I mean to show him very shortly the strength, courage, and fighting skill of the Geats. By the time tomorrow's sun has risen and stands blazing in the south, any man who wishes will be able to go fearlessly into Heorot.'

The king, however, was pleased. When he heard Beowulf's firm resolve, the grey-haired Danish prince felt that he could count upon help.

Laughter and a cheerful din resounded from the soldiers as they talked merrily. Wealhtheow, Hrothgar's queen, now made her appearance according to courtly custom. Adorned with gold, she greeted the company in the banqueting hall. The noble lady first presented a goblet to Hrothgar. She begged him to enjoy the revels, upon which the king gladly took part in the eating and drinking. Then Wealhtheow the Helming princess visited every corner of the hall, tendering the jewelled cup to the veterans and the younger men. The moment came when the gracious lady, wearing her diadem, brought the goblet to Beowulf. She greeted the Geat prince with discreet words, thanking God for the fulfilment of her prayer that she might count upon a hero for help against the attacks. Beowulf received the cup at Wealhtheow's hands. Then, eager for the fight, he made this reply:

'When I set out in my ship to cross the sea with my band of men, it was my intention once and for all to gratify the dearest wish of your people, or to die in the attempt, fast in the grip of the fiend. I shall either perform some heroic feat, or breathe my last in this banqueting hall!'

Wealhtheow was greatly pleased with the confident speech of the Geat. The noble lady, in her golden ornaments, returned to take her seat beside the king.

Then, as before, the brave words of a happy people and

the clamour of a conquering nation resounded in the hall, until presently Hrothgar wished to retire. He knew that the fiend planned to attack the hall as soon as the light of the sun was gone, the night fallen over everything, and dim shapes of darkness came flitting beneath the clouds. The entire company arose. Hrothgar exchanged salutations with Beowulf and wished him good luck and the mastery of the hall. He added these words:

'Since I was able to bear arms I have never entrusted the great hall of the Danes to anyone except, as it now happens, to yourself. Have and hold my great hall; bear in mind your reputation, and show your great strength. Keep a sharp look-out for the enemy. If you emerge alive from this undertaking you shall not want for anything.'

10

HROTHGAR, protector of the Danes, left the hall with his band of men, on his way to bed with Wealhtheow the queen. The word went round that God had set a watch against Grendel in Heorot, and had appointed a man with the special task of guarding the Danish king against monsters. The leader of the Geats was obviously confident in his great strength and in the favour of God. He took off his steel corselet and helmet, giving his patterned sword (which was of the finest metal) to a servant with orders to take charge of his armour. Before lying down on his bed Beowulf made a speech of defiance.

'I do not consider myself to be a fighter inferior either in strength or in experience to Grendel himself; so I shall not kill him with the sword. Although I could do it in that way, that is not how I propose to rid him of his life. He knows nothing of the art of cutting and thrusting, although his

42

murderous exploits are bold enough. Tonight we will do
without weapons, if he really dares to risk a combat with-
out them. God in His wisdom must allot the victory as He
thinks fit.'

With this the hero laid his cheek against the pillow.
Around him many brave seafarers sank to rest in the hall.
Not one supposed that he would ever leave it to revisit his
native land, his family, or the town where he grew up; for
they knew that in the past slaughter had carried off far too
many of the Danes in that banqueting hall. But God gave
the luck of battle to the Geats. He furnished them with
help, so that they all overcame their enemy through the
skill and strength of one man. It is sure that almighty God
has always ruled over the human race.

In black night the prowler of the dark came stalking. The
soldiers who were supposed to defend the gabled hall were
asleep – all except one. It was generally believed that the
fiend could not drag people into the lower shades against
the will of God. Yet Beowulf, keeping an angry watch
against the enemy, waited for the outcome of the battle
with growing fury.

II

Now Grendel, with the wrath of God on his back, came
out of the moors and the mist-ridden fells with the intention
of trapping some man in Heorot. Under the clouds he
strode, until he came in sight of the rich banqueting hall
glistening with plated gold. It was not the first time that he
had paid a visit to Hrothgar's hall; but never before or
afterwards did he experience such bad luck with its defen-
ders. When the unhappy creature approached Heorot, the
door, which was secured with wrought-iron bars, burst

open at the touch of his talons. In his malicious fury he tore
down the entrance of the building. Then the raging fiend,
with horrible firelit eyes, stepped quickly upon the tessel-
lated floor. Inside the hall he saw a great band of brothers-
in-arms sleeping together, at which he laughed to himself,
for the cruel demon, who meant to kill every single one of
them before daybreak, saw before him the prospect of a
huge feast. But after that night it was not his luck to
devour any more people. For Hygelac's mighty kinsman
was watching to see how the marauder would set about his
murderous business.

The fiend wasted no time, but for a start snatched up a
sleeping man. He tore him apart in an instant, crunched the
body, drank blood from its veins, and gulped it down in
great bites until he had wholly swallowed the dead man,
even the hands and feet. Then he advanced nearer. Reach-
ing out with his open hand, the fiend was about to take hold
of the hero on his bed. But Beowulf at once saw the hostile
move and propped himself up on his elbow.[7] The arch-
beast soon realized that nowhere in the world had he ever
met a man with such might in the grip of his hand. Al-
though terror-struck, he could get away none the faster.
He had never met anything like this in his life before; his
one idea was to slink off to his hiding-place to rejoin the
fellowship of devils. But at this point Beowulf remem-
bered the promise which he had made earlier in the even-
ing. He stood upright and gripped Grendel so tightly that
the talons cracked to bursting. The monster fought to
escape, but Beowulf closed with him. The fiend was trying
to break loose and make a bolt for his fen-refuge; yet, as
he knew only too well, his talons were fast in an enemy
clutch. That was a fatal expedition which the demon made
to Heorot. The hall thundered with the hubbub. Every one
of the Danes who lived in the stronghold, soldiers and

chieftains alike, was seized with extreme panic. The furious contestants for the mastery of the hall raged till the building rang. It was a miracle that the beautiful banqueting hall withstood such combatants without falling flat to the ground; but it was firmly braced inside and out with iron clamps forged by skilled craftsmen. They say that where the two antagonists fought, bench after bench inlaid with gold was uprooted from the floor. Till then the most far-sighted among the Danes had never imagined that anybody might wreck their splendid ivory-inlaid hall by ordinary means, or destroy it by dint of cunning (barring fire, which would envelop it in flame). A stupendous din went up. Pure terror laid hold of the Danes, and of everyone outside the hall who heard the howling; the dreadful scream of God's adversary wailing his defeat; the prisoner of hell bellowing over his wound. He was fast in the clutch of the strongest man alive.

12

THE hero had no intention of allowing the murderous visitor to escape with his life, for it was of no use to anyone. Many of Beowulf's followers brandished their ancestral swords [8] to defend, if possible, the life of their beloved leader. When they joined the struggle, meaning to hack at Grendel from every quarter until they found a vulnerable spot, these stout-hearted fighting-men did not realize that no earthly blade or sword of the finest metal could touch the miscreant, who had laid a spell on every kind of edged weapon. His death was to be a miserable one, and his outcast spirit to pass far into the power of devils. It was now that Grendel, the enemy of God who had wantonly committed numberless atrocities against the human race, dis-

covered that his bodily strength was of no use when the
valiant kinsman of Hygelac had got hold of him by the
claw. Neither would give the other quarter. The fiend
suffered excruciating pain. An enormous wound became
visible in his shoulder; his sinews snapped, and tendons
burst. Victory was Beowulf's. Mortally wounded, Grendel
had to take to his heels and make for his wretched home in
the fens with the certainty that his days were numbered and
his life at an end.

By the close of that bloody fight the wish of all the Danes
was fulfilled. It was thus that the resolute, cool-headed man
who had come from a distant land purged Hrothgar's hall
and defended it from attack. The Geat prince rejoiced in his
night's work. For he had made good his boast to the Danes
and put right their trouble, the nightmare (no small afflic-
tion) which they had been forced to suffer. When the hero
set up the talon, arm, and shoulder – Grendel's entire grasp
– under the great gables of Heorot, the evidence spoke for
itself.

13

THE next morning soldiers thronged about the banqueting
hall. Chieftains from all parts near and far travelled over the
highroads to witness the spectacle and to examine the mon-
ster's tracks. His death appeared no cause of regret to those
who saw the creature's trail, which revealed how he had
taken himself off, tired and beaten. The doomed fugitive's
blood-spoor led to a lake of water-demons, boiling with
blood, its terrible waves laced with hot gore. Grendel had
hidden himself there, mortally wounded. Cut off from
happiness, he later gave up his pagan ghost in this fen ref-
uge, where hell received him.

Then the veterans, accompanied by many young men,

returned from their pleasant excursion, trotting back from
the lake on their bay horses. Beowulf's renown was pro-
claimed. Many of them said over and over again that no
other man, north or south, between the seas, anywhere in
the length and breadth of the world or under the sky's ex-
panse, was a better fighter or more deserving of a kingdom.
Yet they did not in the least disparage the good Hrothgar,
their friend and overlord, who was an excellent king.

Now and again they let their horses gallop, racing each
other where the turf tracks appeared suitable or the going
was known to be good. Meanwhile one of the king's chief-
tains, a man with a gift for words, whose mind was stored
with a host of old legends, composed a new poem with cor-
rect versification. Juggling with phrases, he skilfully began
to treat of Beowulf's exploit and soon devised an apt
parallel. He related almost everything (with much that was
new) that he had heard about the remarkable fights and
exploits of Sigemund the son of Waels: [9] his far-flung ex-
peditions and the feuds and treacheries in which he became
involved, which people knew little about. But Sigemund's
nephew Fitela knew, because his uncle had sometimes felt
like discussing them with him; for in all their battles they
had always been friends in need, and had put to the sword
many of the giant race. Much fame ensued for Sigemund
after his death, since that hardy campaigner killed a Worm
which was the guardian of a treasure. Under a grey rock
royal Sigemund attempted this audacious feat on his own.
This time Fitela was not with him. But as it turned out, his
sword drove through the prodigious Worm with such
force that the blade stuck in the rock opposite and the
Dragon was annihilated. By his bravery the hero won the
disposal of as much as he wanted of its treasure. The son of
Waels loaded a ship with it and filled the hold with glisten-
ing gems, while the Worm dissolved in its own heat.

Sigemund prospered in his undertakings and became
easily the best-known adventurer the world had seen since
the decline of the might and daring of Heremod, the Dan-
ish king.[10] During his exile among the Jutes, Heremod had
been betrayed into hostile hands and immediately put to
death. Trouble had fallen heavily and persistently upon
Heremod until he became too heavy a burden to all his fol-
lowers and subjects. Before then many thinking men had
time and again deplored the behaviour of this powerful king.
They were those who had counted on him as a help against
misfortune; who hoped the prince would uphold the
honour of his house and prosperously govern the people,
stronghold, and treasury of Denmark. But whereas evil
took possession of Heremod, Beowulf became dearer to his
friends and everyone else.

Now and again they raced their horses along the sandy
roads. The morning was advanced and already passing.
Many a brave henchman had visited the lofty banqueting
hall to gaze upon the marvellous spectacle. The guardian of
the Danish treasury, the king renowned for noble actions,
emerged magnificently from the bedchamber with a large
bodyguard. Accompanied by the queen with her retinue of
ladies, he took the path to the banqueting hall.

14

As he entered the hall Hrothgar paused on the threshold.
Seeing the tall golden roof-tree and Grendel's claw, he
cried: 'For this sight let thanks be at once offered to the
Almighty! Much horror and distress I have had to suffer at
the hands of Grendel; yet God, who is king of glory, works
miracle upon miracle. It was not so long ago that I gave up
hope of seeing a cure for any of my troubles while this

great building remained soaked in blood. It was an unending grief to my counsellors, who despaired of ever rescuing the hall of my people from fiends and monsters. But now, through the power of the Lord, a man has performed the task which with all our schemings we were so far unable to accomplish. I tell you that the woman who bore such a son into the world may, if she is still living, declare that God was good to her in her childbearing. Now Beowulf, best of men, I will cherish you in my heart as a son. From now on keep to our new relationship. For you, from among what I have, there shall be no lack of the world's goods. It is often enough that I have given a reward for less, and honoured with my gifts a meaner soldier and a lesser fighter. But by your exploits you have established your fame for ever.[11] May God reward you with good fortune, as He has done up to now.'

Beowulf replied: 'When we audaciously took on the might of the unknown we fought and discharged our task with the greatest goodwill. I only wish that you could see the demon himself killed in all his trappings! I meant to pin him quickly to his deathbed in so close a grapple that unless he wriggled his body loose he must fight for life in the grip of my hand. But I could not prevent his escape – God was against it. Hard as I held my enemy, the fiend was too quick for me. However, he left his talon, arm, and shoulder behind, which has saved his life and marked his trail – though the wretched creature has not helped himself in the least thereby. The evildoer is burdened with sins and will live none the longer, because the wound has taken a fatal hold and fettered him with pain. The guilty wretch must now wait for the last judgement, and the sentence of almighty God.'

Then Unferth was less inclined to boast of his warlike deeds when people had seen, hanging from the lofty roof,

the fiend's talon which the prowess of the hero had won.
Each of the finger-tips of the murderous pagan demon –
the places where the nails should have been – was like steel.
Everyone declared that there was nothing hard enough to
sever it and that no sword, however good, could have cut
off the monster's bloodstained claw.

15

ORDERS were immediately given for the decoration of the
interior of Heorot, and a large number of men and women
made the banqueting hall ready. Golden tapestries gleamed
along the walls, and there were many wonderful objects to
be seen by those with an eye for such things. That resplen-
dent building, though secured inside with iron clamps, had
been badly wrecked. The door-hinges were wrenched
away; only the roof was left untouched by the time the
criminal turned and fled in despair of life. Death is not easy
to avoid, try who will. For each living soul on earth must
seek the appointed place, where after the feast of life his
body shall sleep fast in a narrow bed.

The time had come for the son of Healfdene to enter the
hall, because the king himself wished to take part in the
banquet. They say that the Danes never carried themselves
better, or mustered in greater force in the presence of their
sovereign. Men of note took seats on the benches and
regaled themselves with the abundance set before them.
Hrothgar and his valiant nephew Hrothulf toasted one
another with bumpers of mead in the banqueting hall.
Heorot was filled with friends, for as yet the Danes had not
begun to plot against one another.[12]

Hrothgar gave Beowulf an embroidered banner of gold,
a helmet and a corselet, in reward for his victory. Multi-

tudes saw the jewel-studded sword of honour presented to the hero. Beowulf drank a ceremonial cup in the banqueting hall, for the gifts were so costly that in accepting them he need feel no shame before the fighting-men. Few men have presented four such treasures of gold over a banqueting table with so much goodwill. Round the top of the helmet a projecting rim bound with wires guarded the head in such a way that no sword, however sharp and tough, might cripple the wearer when he joined battle with his enemies.[13] In addition Hrothgar ordered eight horses with golden bridles to be led under the courtyard and inside the hall. Upon one was a saddle cunningly inlaid with jewels. This was the king's war-saddle, which Hrothgar used when he went out to battle – and that famous leader never failed to be in the van where the dead fell thickest. The king of the Danes now delivered the horses and weapons into the keeping of Beowulf, and told him to use them well. Thus the renowned prince, guardian of the soldiers' treasury, repaid Beowulf for his combat with Grendel in horses and gold, with a generosity of which every honest man must approve.

16

THE king also presented over the banqueting table some valuable old heirlooms to each of those who had crossed the sea with Beowulf, and ordered a compensation to be paid for the man whom Grendel had wickedly killed. Grendel would have murdered more of them, had not the wisdom of God and the hero's courage saved them from this fate. The Lord ruled over humanity then as he still does today; therefore in every way wisdom and circumspection are best. Whoever lives long in this world must experience much good and evil on this troubled earth.

Songs were sung in Hrothgar's presence to the accompaniment of music. The harp was struck, and many ballads recited. Then, by way of entertainment, Hrothgar's poet sang in the hall of how Hnaef, the leader of a small Danish clan, fell by the hands of Finn's men in a Frisian quarrel, when sudden disaster overtook the Danes.[14] Hnaef's sister Hildeburh, the wife of Finn, had little reason to speak well of the good faith of the Jutes. Through no fault of her own, that skirmish deprived her of those she loved: her son and her brother. One after the other they fell to the spear, till the princess was left heartbroken. Not for nothing did the daughter of Hoc lament that tragic fight. When morning broke she could see in broad daylight the holocaust of her kinsfolk, in whom her greatest happiness in this world had once lain.

However, the battle had made a clean sweep of all except a few of Finn's men, so that it was impossible for him there to give the death-blow to Hengest, Hnaef's second-in-command, or to dislodge his meagre Danish remnant from the hall. So they offered the following terms to the Danes. The Frisians were to make room for them in some other hall with a separate seat of honour, one which the Danes and Jutes could share equally. Further, at the distribution of pay, Finn son of Folcwalda was each day to remember the Danes, and satisfy Hengest's troop with armlets and just as much precious treasure of beaten gold as he intended to give his own Frisians in the banqueting hall. They then concluded on both sides a firm treaty of friendship. Finn swore absolutely and unreservedly to Hengest that he would treat the wretched remainder of the Danish army honourably, according to the decrees of his advisory council. No man was to break the covenant by word or deed. No one was maliciously to remind the Danes that because they were leaderless they must needs follow the man who had killed their chieftain. And if any of the Frisians should rekindle the blood-feud with gibes, then he was to be put to the sword.

A funeral pyre was built and bright gold fetched from the treasury. Hnaef, the Danish hero, was prepared for the funeral pile. Bloodstained corselets, iron helmets with golden boar-crests, and numbers of dead chieftains were plainly to be seen upon the pyre, for many notable men had fallen in battle. Hildeburh gave orders that her own son should be committed to the flames upon Hnaef's pyre and that his body was to be burnt beside his uncle's. The chieftain was placed on the pyre and the princess lamented, keening dirges. The huge funeral flames swirled to the clouds. They roared before the grave-mound, while heads melted, wounds burst open, and blood spurted from gashes in the bodies. Fire, the greediest element, swallowed up the dead on both sides, and their glory perished.

17

HAVING lost their comrades, the soldiers disbanded to their homes and strongholds in Friesland. Hengest, however, stayed behind and lived unhappily at the court of Finn for the whole of an uneasy winter. Although he longed to return home, he could not navigate a ship across the ocean, which foamed with storms and contending winds. Winter locked the waves in fetters of ice until the new year revisited the homes of men, as it does today, with seasonably brilliant spring weather. By the time winter was shaken off and the face of the earth again smiling, the exile was itching to be gone.

But although Finn's guest was eager to quit the hall, yet he thought more of revenge than of the sea voyage. He wondered whether he could bring about some altercation as an excuse to renew the Jutes' acquaintance with his sword. So when Hunlafing laid on Hengest's lap the peerless sword whose edge was so well known to the Jutes, he did not repudiate his obligation to exact vengeance. And when, after their voyage, Guthlaf and Oslaf made a bitter outcry about the surprise attack, blaming Hengest for their misfortunes, he could not control the anger in his heart. So it was then the turn of Finn to suffer in his own home a cruel death by the sword of a foeman. The hall was dyed red with the blood of mortal enemies. In this way King Finn was killed in the midst of his bodyguard, and his queen taken prisoner. The Danish spearmen loaded a ship with all the royal belongings, gems, and jewellery that they could find in Finn's hall. They carried back the noble lady Hildeburh over the sea to Denmark and her people.

The poet's story was told, and the song ended. As mirth renewed and laughter rang out, cup-bearers poured wine from wonderfully made flagons. Wealhtheow now made her appearance. Wearing her golden crown she approached the illustrious pair, Hrothgar and his nephew Hrothulf. There was still peace and good faith between the two. Also present, occupying a place of honour at the feet of the Danish king, was Unferth the orator. Everybody was convinced of his mettlesome spirit and great courage, although he had shown treachery towards his brothers in a passage of arms.

'Take this cup, my lord and king,' said the queen of the Danes. 'Enjoy yourself, generous friend of men, and, as is proper, speak cordially with the Geats. Be open-handed to them, remembering the gifts which have come to you from the ends of the earth. They tell me that you are going to treat this heroic fighting-man as your son. Now that the splendid hall of Heorot is purged, dispense as many gifts as you can while you may, and leave your people and your kingdom to your children when the time comes for you to die! O protector of the Danes, I know my good Hrothulf well enough to be sure that he will take honourable care of our sons if you die before him. And I am sure he will reward our children with good treatment when he remembers all the kindness we lavished upon him to his advantage and delight when he was young.'

With this she turned to the bench where her children Hrethric and Hrothmund sat among a group of youths, all sons of chieftains. Between the two brothers sat Beowulf, the hero of the Geats.

18

THE goblet was brought to him with a friendly invitation to drink, and he was made a generous present of golden metal-work – two armlets, rings, a shirt of mail, and the finest golden collar in the world. They say that nowhere, in any treasury, has there been a richer jewel since Hama carried off to his glittering stronghold the Brosings' necklet together with its precious setting. (Hama fled from Eormenric's hot pursuit and died.) The Geat, Hygelac of the house of Swerting, later took this collar with him on his final expedition, when he had to make a last stand to defend his treasure and booty.[15] He met with his end because he went recklessly in search of trouble, and began a feud with the Frisians. So the great prince, after carrying the treasure and jewels overseas, died shield in hand. Hygelac's body, his armour and the golden collar as well, fell into the hands of the Franks. For when the slaughter was over lesser men looted the dead Geats whose bodies covered the battle-field.

The hall resounded with applause. Wealhtheow said before them all: 'Take this collar, dear Beowulf, and good luck to you, young man. Wear this coat of mail, prosper, and become famous for valour. It is a Danish heirloom. But be a good mentor to my boys, and I will remember to reward you for it. You have behaved in such a way that people everywhere must sing your praises for ever, as widely as the sea which cradles the winds encircles the land. May you flourish as long as you live. I shall rejoice in your prosperity. But be an active friend to my son, you who are now so happy! Here every man is true to one another, good-hearted and loyal to his king; the chieftains are trustworthy, the people alert, and the carousing soldiers obedient to my commands.'

She then returned to her place. The revels ran high and the troops became flushed with wine. They were unaware of the fate which was in store for some of them, once night had fallen and Hrothgar retired to his quarters. As often before, a great company bivouacked in the hall. Benches were cleared away and pillows and bedding spread upon the floor. Among the revellers one whose end was at hand lay down upon his bed a doomed man. At their heads they set their bright shields, and on the bench above each chieftain the towering helmet, corselet of chainmail, and huge spear, were plain to see. It was their practice to be ready to fight at any moment, whether at home or abroad, whenever occasion arose and their commander needed them. They were a fine race.

19

So they fell asleep. But one of them paid a heavy price for his night's rest, as had often happened before when Grendel haunted the banqueting hall and worked his mischief, until the end came and death squared accounts for his wickedness. It became plain to everyone that an avenger had survived the fiend after the struggle. For a woman-monster, Grendel's mother, was brooding over her woes. She was one of the creatures that were forced to live in the icy currents of abominable lakes, because Cain killed his only brother. For this crime Cain had been outlawed, branded a murderer, and made to relinquish human happiness for a lodging in the wilderness. Many doomed beings were descended from Cain, including the detestable outcast Grendel, who found at Heorot a vigilant sentinel waiting to do battle. There the monster had grappled with him, but the man had remembered the wonderful gift of strength given him by God, and trusted the Almighty for grace and help. So he vanquished his adversary and subdued the fiend from hell. Wretched and abashed, the enemy of man had fled from Heorot to seek his deathbed. In spite of that, his mother, hungry and sad at heart, decided to undertake a dismal expedition to avenge the death of her son.

She came to Heorot where the Danes were sleeping in the banqueting hall. Their luck was soon reversed when Grendel's mother burst in, although the terror she inspired was less – just as the fighting strength of a woman is not so great as that of an armed man, when the edges of an inlaid, hammer-beaten and bloody sword bite through the boar-crest on an enemy helmet. Swords were snatched down from above the benches in the hall. Shields were grabbed and lifted up. In the panic nobody thought of helmets or corselets. Once discovered, she was in a hurry to be off to save her skin. She hastily seized one of the chieftains and made for the fens. It was a great fighting-man that she killed sleeping; the counsellor whom Hrothgar loved most in the world. (Beowulf was not there, because earlier on, after the presentation of gifts had taken place, other quarters had been assigned to the noble Geat.) Heorot was in an uproar. She snatched away the famous bloodstained talon. Gloom returned to the hall. But on both sides it was a bad bargain, paid for in the lives of friends.

White-haired old Hrothgar was broken-hearted to learn of the death of his best-loved counsellor. The victorious Beowulf was immediately summoned to his chamber. At daybreak the great champion and his men went to the place where the old king was waiting, wondering whether God would ever grant him a respite from bad news. The beams of the hall thundered as the famous hero crossed the floor with his troop of men. Addressing Hrothgar, Beowulf asked him if the night had been as quiet as he wished.

20

HROTHGAR, protector of the Danes, cried out: 'Do not ask after our well-being! Distress has returned to the Danes. Yrmenlaf's elder brother Aeschere is dead – Aeschere, who was my counsellor and adviser, and my right-hand man when we used to fight for our lives in hand-to-hand scuffles when boar-crested helmets rang! Aeschere was a tested officer, everything that a man should be! Some wandering, murderous fiend has killed him in Heorot, and gone back who knows where with the corpse, gloating triumphantly over its prey. It has avenged the feud wherein you exterminated Grendel in your cruel grip last night, because he had for so long wasted and destroyed my people. He forfeited his life in battle; but now another ravager has come to exact vengeance for its offspring. The feud has been thoroughly avenged, as must appear to many a man who is heartbrokenly lamenting Aeschere, his generous chieftain. The hand which would have given anything that was asked of it now lies dead.

'But I have heard some of my subjects, country people and hall-counsellors, speak of having seen two such enormous monsters haunting the fenland. One of them, so far as they could tell, looked like a woman; but the other, a misshapen brute, trod the wilderness in the form of a man, though his size was greater than a human being's. The country people used to call him Grendel. But they know nothing about his progenitor, or whether any other mysterious beings were begotten before him. They live in an unvisited land among wolf-haunted hills, windswept crags, and perilous fen-tracks, where mountain waterfalls disappear into mist and are lost underground. The lake which they inhabit lies not many miles from here, overhung with groves of rime-crusted trees whose thick roots darken the water. Every night you can see the terrible spectacle of fire on the lake. No one knows how deep it is. Although the antlered hart will sometimes take refuge in that forest after a long chase by the hounds, it will sooner give up its life at the lake's edge than try to escape by plunging in. It is no inviting spot. Frothing waves rise blackly to the clouds when the wind provokes terrifying storms, until skies weep rain in thickening air. Now, again, it is to you alone that we look for help. You still do not know the country, or the terrible place where the criminal is to be found. Seek if you dare! And if you return, I will repay you for the feud as before, with ancient treasures and twisted gold.'

21

BEOWULF son of Ecgtheow replied: 'Venerable king, do not grieve. It is better for a man to avenge his friend than to mourn him long. We must all expect an end to life in this world; let him who can win fame before death, because that is a dead man's best memorial. Rise, King Hrothgar, and let us go at once to pick up the spoor of Grendel's mother. She can go where she likes, but I promise you that she shall find no cover from me, whether in the bowels of the earth, in mountain thickets, or in the depths of the ocean. Have patience in your grief today, as I know you will.'

The old king sprang up and thanked the Almighty for the hero's words. A horse with plaited mane was bridled for Hrothgar, and the prince set out in state, accompanied by a troop of foot. The spoor was clearly visible on the ground and in the forest paths. She had gone straight over the sombre moors carrying the lifeless body of the best chieftain that had held watch in Hrothgar's hall. Over rocky, broken ground the princely company made their way, along meagre tracks, narrow, forbidding bridle-paths, uncertain ways, and beetling crags, past holes of the water-demons. Hrothgar pushed ahead with a few experienced men to find the place. Suddenly he came upon a dismal grove of mountain trees overhanging a grey rock. Below lay the troubled, bloodstained water of a lake.

It was a bitter grief to the Danes, and a shock to each of the chieftains, when they found the head of Aeschere upon a crag overlooking the lake. While they gazed, its waters boiled with blood. At intervals a horn sounded the rally. As the troop rested, they could see swarms of reptiles in the water, and strange dragons groping in the depths; while monsters, serpents, and fierce brutes (like those which, of a morning, sometimes make disastrous forays on the high seas) basked upon the slopes of the cliff. When they heard the sharp blast of the trumpet they scuttled off in fury. With his bow the Geat prince ended the life of one of them as it cut through the waves. His tough war-arrow stuck in its vitals and it swam slower and slower as death overtook it. At once it was fiercely harried with sharp-barbed boar-spears. When it had been subdued by this onslaught, they dragged the prodigious sea-beast out upon the bluff, and examined the ghastly creature.

Beowulf was not in the least afraid of risking his life. He began to put on his princely armour. The great cunningly-woven corselet which shielded his body and so protected his breast that no malicious attack of the fierce demon might endanger his life was now to be put to the proof in the depths of the lake. And the glistening helmet which covered his head, inlaid with gold, hooped with lordly bands, decorated with effigies of boars, exactly as the armourer had long ago and wonderfully made it so that no sword or battleaxe could bite it through, was now to trouble the abyss and penetrate the whirlpool. Not least of these powerful accessories was what Unferth, the king's orator, lent to Beowulf in his need: the sword Hrunting, pre-eminent among ancestral treasures, whose patterned blade was tempered in blood. It had never failed any man who carried it or who dared to undertake bloody exploits on the field of battle. Nor was it the first time that it had been called upon to perform a bold deed. When he lent this weapon to the better fighter, Unferth the mighty son of Ecglaf forgot what he had said before when in his cups. Since he would not risk his life in performing heroic feats beneath the boiling waves, he lost face and forfeited his reputation as a hero. But this was not the case with the other, who had got himself ready for battle.

22

'Wise and generous prince, great son of Healfdene,' said Beowulf, 'now that I am ready to set out, remember what we two said a while ago: that should I lose my life in your service, after my death you would always stand in the place of a father to me. If I die in battle, look after my companions and retainers; and, dear Hrothgar, dispatch to Hygelac the treasures which you gave me. For when the lord of the Geats gazes upon the gold and treasure, he will understand that I have found a good and generous patron and prospered accordingly. Let the illustrious Unferth keep my sharp ancestral sword with the wave-patterned blade. I shall either win fame for myself with Hrunting or perish.'

After this speech the Geat prince set off courageously without so much as waiting for an answer. The tumbling water swallowed him up. It was the best part of a day before he saw the bottom of the lake. But it was not long before the ravening she-beast, who had lorded it for half a century in the waste of waters, realized that someone from above was exploring the monsters' home. She made a lunge and grabbed the hero with her loathsome claws, yet did not wound his body. The chainmail gave him such complete protection that she was unable to penetrate his closely-linked corselet with her horrible talons. When the she-wolf of the water reached the lake floor, she carried the prince off to her den in such a manner that in spite of his courage he was unable to wield his weapons. But swarms of weird beasts assailed him in the depths, pursued him, and tore at his corselet with their ferocious tusks. Then the hero found himself in an enemy hall of some kind, where water no longer troubled him. He was in a vaulted chamber out of reach of the sweep of the torrent, and could see the light of a fire, a brilliant flame brightly gleaming.

The hero could now make out the monster of the lake, an enormous water-hag. His hand did not flinch. He made a great swing at her with his sword, so that the patterned blade sang its hungry battle-cry about her head. But the intruder soon found that his flashing blade was harmless and would not bite. Its edge had failed its master in his hour of need. Yet it had been in many hand-to-hand conflicts and had often split the helmet and pierced the armour of the doomed. For the first time the precious heirloom had failed to live up to its name.

Still resolute, and bearing his reputation in mind, Beowulf did not in the least lose heart. Exasperated, the hero flung down the patterned sword so that it fell stiff and sharp upon the ground. He trusted to his strength and to the might of his hands. This is how a man who hopes to win lasting fame on the field of battle should behave, and not care for his life. The Geat prince did not hesitate, but seized Grendel's mother by the shoulder. In his rage he flung his antagonist crashing to the floor. But she immediately came back at him with a ferocious grapple, closing in till the hero, who was strongest of fighting-men, weakened, stumbled, and took a fall. Then she threw herself on her visitor, unsheathing her broad bright-bladed dagger to avenge her only child. The woven chainmail about his shoulders saved his life by denying entrance to point and edge. Yet the son of Ecgtheow, champion of the Geats, would have perished deep underground if that chainmail corselet had not helped him. For God brought about the victory. Once Beowulf had struggled to his feet, the holy and omniscient ruler of the sky easily settled the issue in favour of the right.

23

DURING the struggle he saw a sword which had won fame in battle. It was a prize weapon, an ancient blade forged by the giants. But for the fact that it was too large for an ordinary man to use in combat, it was a choice weapon; a splendid sword, the handiwork of titans. Raging, berserk, in despair of life, he swung its whorled blade and furiously struck, so that the sword caught her on the neck and slashed clean through her backbone into her doomed body. She fell to the ground, and blood dripped from the sword. The hero rejoiced in his work.

A flame gleamed clearly as the sun in heaven, filling the place with light. He scanned the cavern and turned along the wall. Grim and resolute, Beowulf gripped tight the sword hilt and raised its edge. It was still useful, for he intended to pay back Grendel on the spot for his many raids on the Danes, not to mention the single occasion on which he had killed Hrothgar's retainers in their beds and eaten fifteen of them where they slept, besides carrying off an equal number as booty. The hero had settled that account, and now saw Grendel lying dead and mutilated, just as the fight at Heorot had left him. The corpse bounded up at the sword-stroke, and Beowulf severed its head as it lay lifeless.

The picked men who were watching the lake with Hrothgar presently observed that its turbid water was convulsed and bloodstained. The grizzled veterans conferred about the hero, no longer expecting him to return, for they thought he would be unlikely to come back in triumph to Hrothgar. Most of them concluded that he had been killed by the she-wolf. At the ninth hour Hrothgar went home and the Danes quitted the cliff; but the foreigners stayed on, sick at heart, staring at the lake and hoping against hope to see their friend and chieftain.

Now the fiery blood began to dissolve the sword in iron icicles. It was wonderful how it melted completely away, like ice when the Father who controls the tides and seasons looses the frozen shackles and frees imprisoned waters. He is the true God. Although he could see plenty of treasure there, the Geat prince did not take from the caverns any more spoil than the head and the jewelled sword-hilt. So incandescent was the blood, and so pestilent the fiend which had died, that the sword had already melted; its patterned blade was entirely burnt up. Now that the monster had left this world, the great and weltering expanse of the lake was completely purified.

Presently Beowulf, who had so often furnished protection to seafarers, swam ashore exulting over the great spoil that he had brought with him. His gallant company rushed to meet him, thanking God in their delight at seeing their leader safe and sound. The hero was quickly relieved of his helmet and corselet. Black with blood, the lake subsided under lowering clouds.

Thence they returned rejoicing by the road which they had come. The valiant men hauled the head from the crag with difficulty; no less than four of them laboriously carried to the hall Grendel's head impaled on a spear. Soon the fourteen brave Geats arrived at Heorot, with their leader in their midst striding over the fields to the hall. Crowned with glory, first of heroes, the valiant soldier and intrepid man of action entered to salute Hrothgar. Grendel's head was borne by the hair in front of the Danes and their queen, across the floor of the hall where people were drinking; a fearful and prodigious spectacle.

24

'SON of Healfdene!' exclaimed Beowulf. 'We are glad to bring you these spoils from the lake, spoils which you see here in evidence of our success. I barely escaped with my life from the underwater battle, and it was with difficulty that I engaged in the task. If God had not been my shield, the combat must have come to an abrupt end! I could do nothing with Hrunting in the fight, good weapon though it is. But the Lord, who so often looks after people when they are without friends, allowed me to catch a glimpse of a fine giant sword hanging from a wall. So when I got the chance I drew it and killed the defenders of the place. When the hot blood gushed forth it burnt up the blade; but I carried off its hilt from my opponents, having avenged, as is proper, the persecution and slaughter of the Danes. I promise that you can now sleep carefree in Heorot among your bodyguard and your chieftains, your young men and your veterans; and that you, king of the Danes, need not fear death for your people from that quarter, as you did before.'

With this the golden hilt made by giants in past times was presented to the old king. Thus that remarkable piece of craftsmanship came into the possession of the king of the Danes after the downfall of the demons. Since that malicious fiend, murderous enemy of God, and his mother were both dead, it became the property of the best king of all those who distributed treasure in Scandinavia.

Hrothgar began to speak while he examined the ancient relic, upon which was inscribed an account of the origin of the primeval conflict; how, when the swirling waters of the Flood destroyed the giant race, they suffered sorely; because they were hostile to God, He paid them out with a deluge of waters. On the shining golden guard had been set forth in correct runic lettering the name of the man for whom that choice blade with twisted hilt and serpentine decorations had first been forged. Everyone fell silent when the wise son of Healfdene spoke.

'Listen to me. As an old king whose memory goes back a long way, who has fostered truth and justice among his people, I can tell you that here is the better man. My friend Beowulf, your fame is established everywhere among all peoples. You carry all this great strength of yours with prudence and humility. I shall keep my promise of friendship with you, as we agreed not long ago. You will become a sure and lasting comfort to your nation and a help to mankind.

'How differently Heremod behaved to the Danish people, the children of Ecgwela! He took no pleasure in the happiness, but in the death and destruction of the Danes. Until that infamous king went into solitary exile, far from human happiness, he used to kill his drinking companions and close friends in his paroxysms of fury. Although the Almighty had bestowed upon him, more than anyone else, the enjoyment of power, his mind became increasingly filled with bloodthirsty ideas. He never distributed rings among the Danes, as honour dictates, but lived parsimoniously, and suffered long and painfully for his misdeeds. Learn from this and see what virtue is. Age has made me wise, and I am telling you this for your own sake.

'It is remarkable how almighty God, through His great grace, parcels out wisdom, wealth, and rank amongst mankind. He directs everything. Sometimes He allows the mind of a man of noble race to turn to his native land. He grants him every pleasure in his home, and a well-garrisoned stronghold to defend, while making wide regions of the earth subject to him as well; till in his conceit the man can see no end to it. He lives in luxury, nothing troubles him in the least, neither disease nor age; no annoyance clouds his thoughts, and no hostility arouses enmity against him. The world does as he wants of it, and to him misfortune is a stranger.

25

'But within him arrogance grows and festers. Conscience, which is sentinel of the soul, falls asleep. Surrounded as he is with worldly cares, that sleep is too profound; for a killer is at hand who shoots wickedly from his bow. Then the man is off his guard and is pierced right to the heart by a bitter arrow against which he does not know how to defend himself: the sinister promptings of the Devil. What he has had for so long seems to him not enough. Greedily he covets, and no longer gives away collars of gold, as honour ordains; but instead forgets or pays no attention to the workings of destiny, because of the great blessings which have been heaped upon him by God the king of glory. In the end this is what generally happens. His mortal body (which is doomed to die) perishes, and someone else who is untroubled by his miserly qualms succeeds to the throne and carelessly shares out the man's long-hoarded treasures.

'Be on your guard against such wickedness, my dear Beowulf! Choose the better part, which is eternal gain. Avoid pride, illustrious hero. For a little while you will be at the peak of your strength; but it will not be long before sickness or the sword, or the hand of fire, or the raging sea, a thrust of the knife, a whizzing arrow, or hideous dotage, or failure and darkening of the eyes, will plunder you of your might; and in the end, brave soldier, death will defeat you.

'For example, I reigned over the Danes for half a century and defended them tooth and nail against many nations of the earth, until I did not suppose I had an enemy in the world. See what a reverse of fortune overtook me in my own house, what disasters followed in the steps of success, when the ravaging Grendel became my enemy! Because of his depredations I had to put up with endless anxiety. But, thank God, I have lived to see with my own eyes that hacked and bloody head at the end of a long struggle. Now, crowned with the honours of war, take your seat and enjoy the banquet. You and I will share many treasures in the morning.'

The Geat was pleased, and quickly took his seat as the king directed. An abundant feast was again spread for the soldiers in the banqueting hall.

Dark over the company fell the shadow of night. When the old Danish king wished to retire, the whole gathering rose. To the Geat hero the thought of rest was most welcome. The chamberlain, whose task was to attend to people's wants – such wants as seafarers were likely to have in those days – soon led away the traveller, who was worn out after his adventure.

Where great golden rafters rose above him, the hero fell asleep. The visitor rested there until the black raven cheerfully announced the break of day. Now bright light came chasing the shadows and the troops bustled about. For their chieftains were more than ready to return home, and Beowulf wished to reach his distant vessel.

The hero ordered Hrunting to be brought to Unferth, and begged him to take back his valuable weapon. Beowulf thanked him for the loan, saying that he thought it was an excellent fighting weapon. But, like a generous man, he spoke no word of disparagement concerning the sharpness of its edge.

When his men were equipped and ready, the prince whom the Danes now held in high honour approached the throne where the king was seated. Beowulf, son of Ecgtheow, addressed Hrothgar.

26

'WE sailors from a far country would now like to announce our intention of returning to Hygelac. You have treated us kindly, and we have been entertained here as well as any of us could wish. My lord, I shall always be at hand if by any feat of arms I can earn more of your love than I have so far done. If when I am overseas I should hear of any neighbouring country menacing you as those monsters did a short time ago, I shall bring a thousand fighting-men to your aid. I am sure that Hygelac king of the Geats, young as he is, will encourage me by word and deed to show my regard for you and take my spear and the succour of my strength to your aid, whenever you need men. And should your son Hrethric choose to visit the Geat court, he will find plenty of friends there. Foreign countries are most profitably visited by one who is himself of merit.'

Hrothgar replied: 'God in His wisdom must have put those words into your head. I have never heard anyone so young speak with more discretion. Not only are you great in strength, but mature in understanding and wise in speech. Should war, sickness, or the knife carry off your prince, Hygelac, during your lifetime, I think it unlikely that the Geats will find a better man to elect as their king and guardian of their treasure than yourself, should you wish to rule the kingdom of your ancestors. My dear Beowulf, the better I know your character, the more I like it. You have brought about a mutual peace between our people, the

Geats and Danes. Those wars and feuds which we pre-
viously endured must come to an end. So long as I rule
over this kingdom we shall exchange treasures, friends shall
greet one another with gifts from across the sea, and ships
with curved prows bear presents and tokens of love. I know
that your people are resolute in war as in peace, and their
behaviour impeccable in either case, because they keep to
the old traditions.'

With this Hrothgar, protector of the Danes, gave him
twelve jewels in the hall, begging him to go in peace to his
kinsmen with the treasure and to revisit him soon. Then the
noble king of the Danes clasped the hero round the neck
and kissed him, tears pouring from his grey head. The old
patriarch knew it was improbable they would ever again
meet in high council. Beowulf was so dear to him that he
could scarcely hide his emotion. Deep within his heart a
secret affection for the beloved hero burned in his blood.

Loaded with gold, Beowulf left him, and crossed the
fields exulting over the wealth that he had won. His ship,
riding at anchor, was waiting for her master. While on their
road the Geats sang the praises of Hrothgar's generosity. In
all ways he was an incomparable king, until old age, which
is so often a handicap, took his great prowess away from
him.

27

THE young and heroic band of corseleted fighting-men
soon reached the sea. The coastguard saw their return, just
as he had watched their coming, but this time he did not
challenge them roughly from the headland. Instead he rode
to meet them and said that the Geats would be glad to see
again the soldiers now embarking in their bright armour.

Horses, arms, and gold were brought aboard the great ves-
sel as it lay on the beach, till her mast towered over the
treasure of Hrothgar. Beowulf presented a sword bound
with gold to the officer who had guarded the vessel. Be-
cause of this precious gift the man was more honoured in
the banqueting hall afterwards.

The ship set out, and, furrowing the waves, left the
Danish coast. A spread of canvas was hoisted to the mast
and secured with a sheet. Her timbers thrummed. No head-
wind from sea threw her out of her course; but over ocean
currents shot the curved prow covered with foam, until
they could glimpse the Geat cliffs and familiar headlands.
With a fair wind the boat drove on until she grounded. The
harbourmaster, who had been long and eagerly scanning
the sea for those beloved men, was at once ready by the
water's edge, where, in case the force of the waves should
carry their graceful craft away, he moored the great vessel
to the beach fast by her anchor cables. Beowulf then or-
dered the royal treasure of gold and jewels to be brought
ashore.

Their king was not far to seek, for close to the sea-cliffs
stood the hall where Hygelac, son of Hrethel, and his re-
tainers lived. The building was magnificent, and its prince
valiant. Youthful, wise, and accomplished, Hygd daughter
of Haereth was his queen. Although she had not long been
living in the hall, she was not close-fisted, nor over-miserly
about distributing treasure to the Geats.

How different from that imperious princess Thryth, who
practised unspeakable atrocities! [16] No one of her court ex-
cept her future husband was so bold that he dared look her
directly in the face. For whoever did so could count upon
the death-ropes being prepared for him; and immediately
after his arrest, the sword was brought into play. At one
and the same time the patterned blade announced and per-

formed the sentence of death. For a peacemaker [17] to exact the life of a loyal man on account of some fancied insult is no way for a queen or a woman to behave, however beautiful she may be. But Offa of the house of Hemming put a stop to this. Indeed, it was maintained over the ale-mugs that she was less vindictive and not half so dangerous after she had been given in marriage to that high-born young hero. This happened when at her father's request she sailed over the tawny sea to pay a visit to Offa's court. On his throne she later became celebrated for her goodness, and while she lived made excellent use of her position. She greatly loved the king; who, so they say, was the best of men the wide world over. For Offa, a notable soldier, ruled his native land wisely, and was famous for his victories and generosity. From him sprang Eomer, grandson of Garmund of the house of Hemming, a skilful campaigner and a bulwark of fighting-men.

28

TOGETHER with his companions, Beowulf set out across the wide sandy beaches to the foreshore. The sun that lights the world was hastening from the south. They made their way rapidly to the place where they knew their brave young king (who had been the death of Ongentheow, the Swedish monarch) distributed rings and gold in his stronghold. Hygelac was immediately told of Beowulf's appearance, and informed that the hero, his comrade in arms, had arrived safe and sound in the neighbourhood and was on his way to the hall. By the king's order the banqueting hall was at once made ready to receive the travellers.

When he had formally and ceremoniously saluted his sovereign, the hero home from the wars took his seat beside the king; for they were kinsmen. Queen Hygd, who loved her people, went round the hall with vessels of mead, and placed goblets in the hands of the fighting-men. Hygelac began courteously to question his friend in the banqueting hall, since he was burning with curiosity to hear what adventures had befallen the Geats.

'How did things go with you on your expedition, my dear Beowulf, when you suddenly took it into your head to go looking for trouble overseas, and fight in Heorot? Have you at all relieved the notorious suffering of Hrothgar? At heart I was very anxious and sad, because I had no faith in my dear friend's undertaking. I begged you long and earnestly to go nowhere near that murderous fiend, but to let the Danes settle their feud with Grendel by themselves. Thank God, I say, that I am allowed to see you safe and sound.'

Beowulf replied: 'King Hygelac, already many people have heard about the great fight between me and Grendel in the place where he inflicted such endless miseries upon the Danes. I have avenged them all, so none of Grendel's kind on earth, not even the longest-lived of that loathsome, criminal pack, may boast about that midnight battle.

'When I arrived I went straight to the hall to salute Hrothgar, who seated me beside his own sons as soon as he understood what I proposed to do. All were enjoying themselves; in fact I never saw so much gaiety in any banqueting hall. His noble queen, who is a pledge of peace between the Danes and Helmings, went the rounds of the hall every now and then, urging the young men to eat and drink, sometimes presenting a gold ring to one of the soldiers before she retired to her seat. Sometimes Hrothgar's daughter carried goblets of ale to the senior chieftains in succession – as she handed the flagon round I heard people call her Freawaru. Young and adorned with gold, she was

74

promised in marriage to Froda's good-looking son, Prince
Ingeld of the Heathobards. King Hrothgar arranged it, and
thinks it a good plan to end the many bitter feuds between
the Danes and the Heathobards through this girl. But after
the death of a prince it seldom happens that the spear lies idle
for long, however beautiful the bride may be.

'For it may gall Prince Ingeld, and every man of his race,
when he enters the banqueting hall with his bride, that the
treasures of the Heathobards, the arms and armour that
their ancestors once wielded, should glitter upon the backs
of her Danish retainers now being banqueted.

[29]

'BUT in the battle the Heathobards had led their comrades,
as well as their own lives, to destruction. Sooner or later,
when drinking has begun, some fierce old spearman who
remembers everything, including the massacre of his com-
rades, will recognize one of the swords. In bitterness of
heart he will begin to sound some young fellow and stir up
trouble with talk like this: "My friend, can you recognize
that weapon which your own father last carried into battle,
when these brave Danes killed him and held the field after
the death of Withergyld and the destruction of our men?
Now the son of one of his killers is swaggering in his
armour in our banqueting hall, bragging of that slaughter
and flaunting a sword which by rights should be yours."
In this manner he will egg him on at every turn, and lash
him with blistering words, until the day shall come when
one of Freawaru's Danish retainers, drenched in blood
from a sword-thrust, forfeits his life for what his father
did; while the man who killed him escapes because he
knows the neighbourhood. Then on both sides the oaths

of the chieftains will quickly be broken. Bitter hatred must
swell in Ingeld's breast, while, owing to his anguish of
mind, his love for his wife must cool. That is why I do not
think much of this friendship of the Heathobards, or con-
sider the peace treaty with the Danes to be either real or
lasting.

'Now I will tell you more about Grendel, so that you,
my lord, can understand what really happened in the fight.
After sunset the angry demon, who was at his worst during
the hours of darkness, came looking for us where we, as yet
unscathed, kept watch in the banqueting hall. The en-
counter turned out to be a disastrous one for Hondscioh,
who was fated to meet a violent end. He was first to fall.
Grendel proved a greedy killer to my dear comrade, for he
gobbled up his entire body. With blood dripping from his
fangs, even then the murderer was so bent upon destruction
that he refused to leave the hall empty-handed. He took me
on with that vast strength of his, and seized me in his eager
claw. He dangled an enormous and extraordinary glove
secured with weird clasps and made with demoniac skill
from the skins of dragons.[18] The fiend was going to stow
me, and many more, into it, though I had done nothing to
provoke him. But he could not manage to do so, for I
sprang up in fury. It would take too long to tell how I
settled accounts with this public enemy for every single one
of his crimes; but what I did, my lord, redounded to the
credit of your people. He escaped to enjoy the sweets of
life a little longer; but his right hand remained behind in
Heorot while he sank miserably to the bottom of a lake.

'Next day, when we sat down to banquet, the king of
the Danes rewarded me generously for this encounter, with
treasures and beaten gold. Songs and junketing followed,
and the patriarch Hrothgar, who had a great fund of
stories, told anecdotes about bygone times, and every now

and then played a pleasant melody on the harp. Now and then some true and unhappy ballad was sung; occasionally the king would recount a curious legend in its correct form; or sometimes, feeling bowed down with age, he would lament his lost youth and vanished prowess in battle. The old man was deeply moved when he remembered so much.

'So we enjoyed ourselves the livelong day, until another night fell upon us. But by now Grendel's mother was burning for revenge, and bore down on us full of bitterness because death and the enmity of the Geats had taken her son. The hag avenged her child by slaughtering a chieftain. Aeschere, an experienced counsellor, lost his life. But in the morning the Danes could neither burn his dead body nor lay their comrade upon his pyre, because she had carried off the corpse in her fiendish clutch under the mountain torrent. This was the worst grief of all for Hrothgar. The king sadly begged me, for your sake, to exhibit my prowess and win fame at the risk of my life in the raging depths; for which he promised me reward. There, as you know, I lit upon the grisly guardian of the abyss. For some time it was a hand-to-hand fight. The waves boiled with blood; and with a giant sword I cut off the head of Grendel's mother in her den. I barely escaped with my life. But my hour had not yet come, and Hrothgar son of Healfdene once more loaded me with gifts.

31

'THE king kept good customs, and I by no means lost the reward for my prowess. For Hrothgar gave me my pick of treasures, which I will bring to you, my lord, and gladly lay before you. My whole happiness still depends on you, and apart from yourself, King Hygelac, I have few near relatives.'

Then Beowulf commanded a great standard with the boar's-head crest, a towering war-helmet, a steel corselet, and a glittering sword to be brought in. He said, 'The venerable king Hrothgar gave me this armour and particularly requested me to tell you its history. He said that Heorogar, the Danish king, owned it for a long time, but none the less would never grant the corselet to his own child, the valiant Heoroweard, although he was a loyal son to him. Use it well!'

Following close upon the armour came four swift bay horses exactly alike. Beowulf presented Hygelac with the horses and armour. This is the way in which kinsmen ought to behave, instead of weaving dark and subtle conspiracies against one another, or plotting each other's death. Hygelac's nephew Beowulf was thoroughly loyal to him: and each kept the other's good in mind. It is said that Beowulf presented Hygd with the curiously-made necklet which Queen Wealhtheow had given him, as well as three graceful horses with gleaming saddles. When the presentation of gifts was over she wore it on her breast ever afterwards.

Through noble actions Beowulf showed his quality. He behaved honourably and with discretion. Nor, in his cups, did he ever kill his drinking-companions; for he was not bloody-minded, but kept for its proper use in battle the precious gift that God had given him – greater skill than any other man. Yet he had been looked down upon for a long time. The Geats had not thought he was courageous, nor did their king suppose him to be worthy of any particular distinction in the banqueting hall, for they imagined that he was a slack and weak young prince. But the famous hero won compensation for every slight. The king now commanded Hrethel's golden heirloom to be brought in. Among the Geats at that time there was no greater treasure in the way of a sword. Hygelac laid it in Beowulf's lap, and gave him a hall and 7,000 hides of land. Thus both had large ancestral estates in that country; but Hygelac's were the greater, as befitted his higher rank.

In later days, through the fortune of war, it came about that Hygelac was killed. And in spite of protecting shields, his son Heardred also fell by the sword. The Swedes, who were formidable fighting-men, sought out Heardred among his bodyguard and attacked him in force. It followed that the great kingdom of the Geats came into the hands of Beowulf. He ruled it well for half a century. But when he was an aged and veteran king, a certain Dragon began to exert its power in the darkness of night. In its upland lair it kept guard over a treasure in a huge funeral barrow, under which ran a secret passage.[19] Some man wandering near that pagan hoard found his way in and stole a great jewelled cup. The Dragon, tricked by a thief's cunning while it slept, made its loss known; and the neighbourhood soon discovered how enraged it was.

32

THE man who so provoked the Worm did not violate its treasure wilfully or on purpose, but through sheer necessity. He was a slave belonging to somebody or other, and was running away from a beating. This guilty fellow, being in need of shelter, had forced his way in. Stark terror took hold of the intruder the moment he entered, but nevertheless the fugitive, when the sudden peril came upon him, escaped from the Worm and took to his heels with a jewelled cup.

Many such ancient treasures lay in the tumulus, where in times gone by an unknown man had carefully hidden the immense ancestral wealth of some great race. All had long been dead; and the chieftain who survived them, disconsolate at the loss of his kinsmen, supposed that, like them, he would possess their slowly gathered wealth for a short time only. Ready to hand upon a cliff near the sea stood a newly completed barrow, which had been fortified to make it impregnable. Into this the guardian of the hoard had carried rings and beaten gold, the richest part of the treasure. He said:

'Earth, hold what men could not, the wealth of princes. For heroes won it from you long ago. The holocaust of battle has claimed every mortal soul of my race who shared the delights of the banqueting hall. I have none to wield the sword, none to polish the jewelled cup. Gone are the brave. The tough helmet, overlaid with gold, must be stripped of its golden plates. They sleep who should burnish the casques. Armour that stood up to the battering of swords in conflict, among the thunder of the shields, moulders away like the soldier. Nor shall the corselet travel hither and yon on the back of a hero by the side of fighting-men. There is no sweet sound from the harp, no delight of music, no good hawk swooping through the hall, no swift horse stamping in the castle yard. Death has swept away nearly everything that lives.' [20]

In this fashion the one survivor sadly lamented, wandering mournfully about night and day, till death touched his heart.

The treasure in the open barrow was found by the primeval enemy that haunts the dusk: the scaly, malicious Worm which seeks out funeral mounds and flies burning through the night, wrapped about with flame, to the terror of the country folk. Its habit is to seek out treasure hidden in the earth and mount guard over the pagan gold; but, though ancient in years, it will profit nothing thereby. Thus for three centuries this public scourge watched over its subterranean treasure, until a certain man lashed it into fury by taking a golden cup back to his master as a peace-offering. Then the hoard was ransacked and the store of jewels plundered. The wretch's petition was granted when his master saw for the first time that ancient craftsmanship.

When the Worm awoke, the trouble began. It slid implacably over the rocks, and picked up the track of the enemy who had come so close to it with such stealthy cunning. (Which shows how a man whose hour has not yet come, and whom the favour of God protects, may easily survive grief and banishment.) The keeper of the treasure-hoard cast eagerly about to find the man who had done it such mischief while it slept. It circled the barrow again and again, burning with anger, but nobody was to be seen in that deserted spot. Thirsty for revenge, it repeatedly went back to the mound to look for that precious cup. Some human being had obviously been tampering with the treasure. The monster, swelling with exasperation, impatiently waited for night to fall, when the theft of the cup could be repaid with fire. To the delight of the Worm, the day drew to a close. It had no wish to stay in the tumulus, but flashed forth armed with flame. That was a bad beginning for the people of that land; but soon there was a worse ending for their king.

33

THE creature began to spew fire and burn dwellings; and while the light of burning filled people with horror, the flying monster spared no living thing. The onset and devastating vengeance of the Worm, its hatred for and humiliation of the Geats, was to be seen everywhere. Before daybreak it flew back to its secret hide-out, the treasure-hoard, having surrounded the country-folk with fire and flame and burning. It trusted to its own ferocity and in the ramparts of the barrow, yet that faith proved deceptive.

To Beowulf was quickly brought the crushing news that the great building which was both his home and the royal hall of the Geats had been burnt to the ground. This was a bitter blow and a severe trial to the hero. Imagining that he had greatly angered the Lord through some breach of the commandments, he became prey to gloomy thoughts, which was contrary to his usual habit.

But when the fiery Dragon razed the national stronghold and the seaboard, the king of the Geats planned to take vengeance. He gave orders for the construction of a wonderful shield made entirely of iron, for he was well aware that a wooden buckler would be of no use against fire. Both the king, whose worth had long been manifest, and the Worm which had watched over its treasure-hoard for so many ages, were to quit this world together. Yet the king disdained to hunt out the marauder with an army, for he did not fear to fight it, nor did he rate the might and valour of the Worm highly. Since purging Hrothgar's hall and crushing the loathsome family of Grendel, he had been in plenty of tight corners and had survived many a hard tussle.

Not least of his hand-to-hand combats was that in which Hygelac was killed. The king of the Geats fell to the sword in a mêlée during a battle in Friesland. But Beowulf escaped through his great strength and prowess as a swimmer. He carried thirty corselets over his arm when he plunged alone into the sea. The shield-bearing Hetware who attacked him had small cause for self-congratulation over this skirmish, seeing how few came home alive from that great fighting-man.

Alone and wretched, Beowulf swam across the expanse

of the sea and returned to his own people. Queen Hygd offered him the treasury and kingdom, throne and exchequer, because she did not think that her child Heardred would be able to defend the ancestral hall against a foreign army now that Hygelac was dead. But the bereaved nation could not persuade Beowulf to become Heardred's overlord on any conditions whatever, or to consent to accept the throne. Instead he supported Heardred in public with friendly and respectful advice until he grew older and reigned over the Geats.

Then Eanmund and Eadgils, banished sons of Ohthere, fled across the sea to Heardred because they had rebelled against their uncle Onela (the greatest of the sea-kings of Sweden). This brought about the death of Heardred, whose hospitality earned him a mortal wound from the sword of Onela. After the death of Heardred, Onela withdrew to his own land and allowed Beowulf to occupy the throne and rule the Geats. He made an excellent king.

34

IN later years Beowulf was careful to take revenge for the king's death. He made friends with the destitute Eadgils, and backed him with arms and men in an overseas expedition. After a grim campaign Eadgils obtained vengeance and killed Onela. Thus Beowulf had survived all battles, feuds, and heroic undertakings, until the day came on which he was to fight the Worm.

Filled with anger the king of the Geats and eleven others set out to find the Dragon. By now Beowulf had learnt the cause of the feud which was so disastrous to his people. For the famous cup had come into his possession, having been given to him by the finder, who made the thirteenth man of the party. This was the miserable serf who had started the whole trouble, and who was forced to lead them humbly to the spot. Willy-nilly he had to go to the place where the barrow was situated. The subterranean vault, packed with jewels and twisted gold, stood near the rolling sea, where its ghastly primeval sentinel watched over the underground hoard; no easy prize for anyone to carry off.

Upon a headland the king of the Geats halted while he said farewell to his followers. His mind was uneasy and restless, anticipating the end. The doom which was to attend the old hero, probe the resources of his soul, and tear the life from his body, was close at hand. Not much longer would flesh enclose the spirit of the king. Beowulf son of Ecgtheow exclaimed:

'In my youth I came safely through many a battle, many a time of war. I remember them all. When I was seven years old the brave and generous king Hrethel of the Geats took me from my father. He gave me board and supplied me with money, and did not forget our blood-relationship.[21] While he lived, I, as one of the men in his stronghold, was treated just the same as his own sons – Herebeald, or Haethcyn, or my own Hygelac.

'But through bad luck the eldest was laid on his deathbed by his brother's fault. For Haethcyn struck down his friend and liege with an arrow from his bow. He missed his aim and shot his brother Herebeald. One brother killed the other with a bloodstained shaft! This was an inexpiable accident, and a heartrending crime; for whatever happened, Herebeald must die unavenged.[22]

'It was just as harrowing as the case of some old man who lives to see his young son swinging on the gallows.[23] He laments his child, who is strung up as food for ravens, with dirges; yet being old can do nothing to help, and each day is continually reminded of the death of his son. He

does not want to live to see another heir in his stronghold
when the first has felt death's sting. It breaks his heart to
look upon his son's dwelling-place, the empty banqueting
hall which is now cheerless and a home of winds. The horse-
men and the men-at-arms sleep in their graves. The harp
makes no sound, and in the courts there is no longer joy.

35

'So he takes to his couch, where the lonely may lament the
lost. To him his lands and dwelling seem too spacious.

'Just so was Hrethel heartbroken over Herebeald. But
although he had no love for Haethcyn, he could not bring
himself to pursue him and make the murderer pay the
price. This sorrow weighed on him so heavily that he
abandoned all hope of happiness and died. Yet when he
departed, he bequeathed his stronghold and kingdom to
his two remaining sons, like any prosperous man.

'But after the death of Hrethel, bickering between the
Swedes and the Geats gave rise to a bitter overseas war. The
sons of the Swedish king Ongentheow became pugnacious
and refused to keep the peace, but kept springing ambus-
cades round about Hreosnaburg. As is well known, my
kinsmen Haethcyn and Hygelac exacted vengeance for
these outrages, though one of them had to pay for it with
his life, which made it a hard bargain. For the fight proved
fatal to Haethcyn king of the Geats. But next day, as we
know, Hygelac obtained vengeance for his brother, whose
killer, Ongentheow the Swedish monarch, fell beneath the
sword when he attacked Eofor the Geat. His helmet was
split apart, and the old Swedish king fell mortally wounded.
Eofor's hand remembered injuries enough and did not
shrink from dealing the death-blow.

'And it was given me to repay with my bright sword on the field of battle the treasures, homestead, and estates which Hygelac lavished upon me. He had no need to hire lesser champions from among the Gifthas, Danes, or Swedes, when I was ever in the van of the army. There I shall always fight so long as this sword lasts, the sword which has served me well at all times, ever since my prowess brought about the death of Daeghrefn, the champion and standard-bearer of the Franks. Daeghrefn was not able to carry off his spoil to the Frisian king, for, in the pride of his strength, he fell in battle – but not to the sword; it was my terrible grip that splintered every bone in his body and stopped the beating of his heart. Now my hand and the edge of my sword must do battle for the treasure-hoard.'

Making defiance for the last time, Beowulf went on: 'I fought many battles when I was young. Yet although I am now an aged king, I shall once more go out to fight and win renown – if the creature will only come out of its burrow to meet me.' Then he addressed each of his men, who were all his close friends, for the last time. 'I would not take a sword or any kind of weapon against the Worm if I knew how else I could honourably come to grips with the monster, as I did long ago with Grendel. But as I expect to meet a poisonous blast of flame I am carrying a shield and corselet. I shall not yield an inch to the guardian of that treasure-hoard. But upon that rampart fate, the master of us all, must decide the issue. My mind is made up; therefore I shall cut short my boasts against the Dragon.

'You soldiers, protected by your corselets, may watch from this hill to see which of us can best stand his wounds by the end of the combat. It is not your business nor any man's but mine to measure strength with the monster and win renown. By my own might I shall obtain the gold, or battle will claim your king.'

With this the hero, leaning on his shield, rose to his feet. In helmet and corselet he advanced to the foot of the jagged cliff, trusting to his own strength. This was not a coward's behaviour. And now that man of supreme merit, who had survived so many wars and pitched battles with foot-soldiers clashing, caught sight of the stone arches in the wall of the tumulus, from which issued a swirling exhalation of flame, so hot that no one could enter without being roasted. The king of the Geats roared a furious challenge. He shouted until his voice penetrated the cavern and his battle-cry thundered under the grey rock. The guardian of the treasure-hoard bristled with rage when it recognized the voice of a man. There was no time for appeasement. The monster's scorching breath spurted ahead of it, out of the rock, while earth reverberated. The hero, facing the barrow, swung his shield to meet the enemy; upon which the reptile was spurred to take the offensive. Already the king had drawn his sharp ancestral sword. But each of the adversaries was in awe of the other. The prince resolutely stood his ground in the shelter of his great shield while the Worm gathered its coils together. Bent like a bow, the flaming monster hurtled towards him and rushed upon its fate. But the king's shield gave protection to life and limb for a shorter time than he had hoped. For the first time Beowulf had to fight without success, because fate refused to grant it to him. Raising his hand, the lord of the Geats struck the glittering monster with his sword, but the blade bounced off the scales and scarcely bit, just when the king had most need. The blow infuriated the guardian of the barrow. It spat a blast of glistering fire which leapt hither and thither. The king could boast of no advantage now that his naked blade had failed him in battle, as no good sword should do. It was no easy thing for Beowulf to make up his mind to quit this world and take up his lodging in some other, whether he liked it or not. But this is the way in which everyone has to die.

Soon the antagonists joined battle once more. The Dragon had taken fresh heart and found its second wind, while the king, hedged round with fire, suffered agony. His comrades-in-arms, who were sons of princes, utterly failed to support him in strength like good fighting-men, but fled into a wood to save their lives. Yet one among them was pricked by conscience. To a right-thinking man, blood must always be thicker than water.

36

HIS name was Wiglaf son of Weohstan, a well-liked Swedish prince of the house of Aelfhere. Wiglaf could see that the king, in spite of his armour, was in distress from the flames. And when he remembered those favours which Beowulf had showered upon him – the rich hall of the Waegmundings, with all the rights that his father had enjoyed – he could hold back no longer, but gripped his yellow shield with one hand while the other drew his ancestral sword.

This weapon was known to have belonged to a son of Ohthere – the banished Eanmund, whom Wiglaf's father Weohstan had killed in battle and stripped of his bright helmet, ringed corselet, and huge sword, which he handed over to Onela, the Swedish king. Onela granted Weohstan the war-equipment and fighting-gear of his nephew Eanmund, all in perfect condition. No mention of a blood-feud was made, although Weohstan had killed Onela's brother's son. So for many years Weohstan kept his booty, until his son Wiglaf came to man's estate like his father before him. Then Weohstan, before his death at a ripe old age, bestowed upon him in the presence of the Geats a great quantity of war accoutrements of every kind.

Now this was the first occasion on which Wiglaf had followed his king into battle. But his courage did not waver, nor did his father's sword fail him in combat, as the Worm was to find out when they encountered one another.

In bitterness of heart Wiglaf reminded his comrades of their duty. 'I can remember a time when we used to accept mead and payment in the banqueting hall from our king, to whom we swore that if ever he fell into straits like these we would make some return for our fighting-gear – these swords and helmets. That is why he decided to pick us out of his whole army for this adventure, thinking that we deserved the honour. That is why he gave me valuable gifts, and you as well. He thought that we were brave spearmen and daring soldiers. Yet because he has performed greater and more desperate exploits than any man, our king and protector intended to accomplish this heroic task by himself. But now the time has come when our leader requires the help of brave men. However scorching that fire may be, let us go forward to our king's assistance. God knows that so far as I am concerned I would much prefer the flame to swallow up my body with my king and benefactor. To my way of thinking it is dishonourable for us to take our shields home without first killing the enemy and saving the king's life. I am sure that this is not what he deserves for his past exploits, that of all us Geats he alone should suffer and die. Let us share the battle with Beowulf.'

Then he dived into the perilous smoke, bearing arms to the king's help and crying: 'Dear Beowulf, make good the vaunt which you made in your youth – that so long as you were alive you would never allow your glory to tarnish! Brave prince, renowned for feats of arms, defend your life with all your might – I am coming to your help!'

At these words the Worm angrily emerged once more in swirls of sparkling flame, to take the field against its enemies, the human beings which it hated. Wiglaf's shield was burnt to the boss by a cataract of fire, while his corselet gave him no protection. The lad slipped quickly behind his kinsman's shield as soon as the flames had burnt his own to cinders.

But the king was still mindful of his fame and struck so hard with his sword that, driven by the impetus, it stuck square in the Dragon's head. Yet Beowulf's patterned sword, Naegling, failed him. It shivered to splinters. Never had it been his luck that a sword should be of use to him during a fight. His hand, they say, was so strong that the force of his blows overtaxed any weapon. Even when he carried one which was hardened in battle he was no better off.

The flame-spitting Dragon screwed up its courage for a third attack. When it saw its chance it set savagely upon the hero, catching him around the neck with lacerating fangs. A torrent of gore gushed out, and Beowulf was spattered with his own life-blood.

37

BUT we are told that in the king's extremity his kinsman Wiglaf displayed his inherited skill and daring. Though he was protected by his armour, the brave fellow's hand was severely scorched in helping his kinsman; by not aiming at the head, he struck the creature slightly lower. His golden sword plunged in with such effect that from that moment the fire began to abate. Collecting his wits, the king pulled out a razor-sharp dagger which he wore at his corselet, and ripped open the belly of the Worm. Together the kinsmen killed their adversary. That is how a man should act in a tight corner! It was Beowulf's crowning hour of triumph, his last feat of arms, and the end of his life's work.

For the wound which the Dragon had just inflicted upon him began to burn and swell. Beowulf soon discovered that mortal poison was working in his breast and had bitten deep into his entrails. Brooding, the king moved to a seat beside the rampart, where he could view that work of giants and survey the stone vault firmly based on pillars within the ancient tumulus. With his own hands the trusty Wiglaf undid his helmet and bathed with water his friend and lord, who was exhausted and soaked in blood from the battle. In spite of his pitiful wound, Beowulf began to speak. He knew well enough that his span of life and term of happiness on earth was over, his sum of days wholly spent, and death very close.

'I now would wish to hand over my armour to a son of mine, were it my luck to have had an heir of my body to come after me. I have reigned over this people for half a century, and there was not a king of any neighbouring nation who dared to attack me with an army or to threaten me with war. The destiny allotted to me on earth I endured; what was mine I defended well. I did not pick quarrels nor swear false oaths. Though wounded to death, I can rejoice in all these things; because when the life quits my body God cannot accuse me of the murder of my kin. Dear Wiglaf, since the Worm lies dead and sleeps mortally hurt, its wealth taken from it – go quickly now and find the treasure-hoard under the grey rock. Now hurry, that I may see that golden treasure and properly examine those shining gems, so that through the richness of the hoard I may more easily relinquish my life and the kingdom which I have long ruled.'

38

WHEN Wiglaf heard these words he obeyed his maimed and wounded king without delay. Corseleted, he entered the vault under the barrow. When he had gone past the seat outside he exultantly took stock of the priceless jewels and gleaming gold that littered the floor, and the wonderful things hanging from the walls. Gazing upon the den of the Worm, the old night-flier, he perceived vessels standing uncared-for, with their decorations dropping off – the drinking-cups of some bygone race; many a rusty old helmet and many a cunningly twisted arm-band. Treasure or buried gold can easily get the better of a man, even if he hides it. He also saw a wonderful piece of craftsmanship hanging high above the treasure-hoard: a golden banner woven by skilful hands. Light flashed from it, so that he could discern the ground and survey the treasure. There was no trace of the Worm, for it had perished by the sword.

It was in this way, according to the tale, that one man rifled the riches of the tumulus, the primordial work of giants. Wiglaf piled into his bosom the goblets and dishes that caught his fancy, and took the golden banner as well. The old king's iron sword had scotched the creature that had long been keeper of the treasure, to guard which it had spat fire of nights until it met with a violent death. Spurred by his booty, the messenger hastened to get back, tormented by misgiving as to whether he would find the weakening king of the Geats alive where he had left him. Loaded with treasure, he at length found his lord and master, bleeding and at his last gasp. Wiglaf began to dash water over him until words forced their way to the hero's lips. The old king looked sadly at the gold, and said:

'I speak with words of thankfulness to God the king of glory, our eternal Lord, for all the wealth that I see here, and because I was permitted to win it for my people before my death. Now that I have bartered my worn-out life for the treasure-hoard, look after my people. I can stay here no longer. When the funeral fire is over, command my chieftains to build upon a headland near the sea a splendid tumulus, which shall tower high over Hronesness to keep my memory green among my people; so that seamen who steer their great ships far over the misty sea may call it Beowulf's Barrow.'

The great-hearted king undid the golden collar from his neck, and gave it with his golden helmet, corselet, and ring to the young spearman, telling him to use them well.

'You are the last survivor of our family, the house of the Waegmundings. Fate has swept away the courageous princes who were my kinsmen, and I must follow them.'

This was the old king's last utterance before committal to the rolling flames of his funeral pyre. The soul left his body to seek the reward of the just.

39

It was a bitter moment for Wiglaf when he surveyed that most loved hero wretchedly dying on the ground. The Dragon that had killed him was also lying there, crushed and lifeless. No more would the coiled Worm guard the hoarded treasure, for keen blades of hammered iron had destroyed it. The far-flying one had been mortally wounded, tumbled to earth beside its treasure-house. No more would it spin through the air at dead of night to flaunt itself in its possession of the treasure, for the hand of the king had felled it to the ground. Legend says that no champion in the

land, however audacious, had ever braved the poisonous
blast of the creature's breath or laid a finger on the gold,
when he found its guardian at home and on the alert in the
tumulus. But Beowulf paid with death for the princely
hoard. He and the Dragon died together.

Soon the deserters came out of the wood: all ten of the
cowardly runaways who had not had the courage to lift a
spear when their leader was in difficulties. In shame they
carried their shields to the place where the old hero lay, and
looked at Wiglaf. Worn out, he was sitting by the shoulder
of his lord, trying without success to revive him with
water. Much as he wished, he could not keep life in the
king, or change the will of the Almighty. The judgement
of God controlled the doings of everyone just as it does
today. The young champion promptly delivered a bitter
rebuke to the men who had lost their nerve. Wiglaf son of
Weohstan gazed in sadness at those whom he no longer
loved, and said:

'Listen. Anyone who cares to speak the truth can say
that the king who gave you the valuable arms which you
now bear – when he used to present to his retainers over his
banqueting table the best corselets and helmets to be found
anywhere in the world – utterly squandered all that armour.
For when it came to fighting, the king was given no reason
to boast of his comrades-in-arms. However, the God of
victories allowed him to avenge himself single-handed with
his own weapon when courage was needed. Though I could
give little protection to his life, yet I went to help my kins-
man as far as lay in my power. When I struck the Dragon
a blow with my sword it weakened, and fire abated from
its fangs. Too few defenders thronged about their king in
his time of trial! Now the receiving of treasure, the giving
of swords, and every enjoyment of home and happiness
must cease for you and your families. As soon as the princes

of all nations hear about your flight and your shameful
conduct, each of your clan will go landless and destitute.
To any fighting-man death is better than a life of dis-
honour.'

40

THEN he ordered the result of the battle to be made known
in the fort upon the sea-cliff, where for a whole morning
chieftains and men-at-arms had been gloomily waiting to
hear whether the hero was dead or on his way home. The
messenger who rode up the hill did not keep back the
news, but told them frankly to their faces:

'The beloved king of the Geats now lies stiff upon his
deathbed. That he rests on a field of slaughter is the work
of the Worm. But though his sword could not make the
least wound in the monster, his adversary lies beside him
dying from dagger-wounds. Wiglaf son of Weohstan is
remaining with Beowulf, a living hero beside the dead.
In sadness and distress he is keeping watch over the man
we love and over our enemy.

'Our country may now expect a time of war as soon as
the king's death becomes known to the Franks and the
Frisians. For when Hygelac sailed with his fleet to the
Frisian land, where the Hetware attacked him, a bitter feud
was begun. Their superior strength brought about Hyge-
lac's downfall. Instead of sharing the loot with his captains,
our leader died among his fighting-men. Ever since then
the king of the Franks has been unfavourably disposed to
us.

'I do not count upon any peace or good faith on the part
of the Swedes either. For, as everybody knows, the Swedish
monarch Ongentheow killed king Haethcyn son of Hrethel

at the battle of Ravenswood when the Geat people made
their first attack on the Swedes for their arrogance. The
veteran Ongentheow, father of Ohthere, was prompt with
his counterblow. He killed king Haethcyn and rescued his
own wife, the aged queen, mother of Onela and Ohthere,
who had been robbed of her gold. Then he gave chase to
his enemies the Geats, until they barely managed to escape
leaderless into Ravenswood. With a huge army he then
besieged the wounded and exhausted remnant. All through
the night he promised destruction to the wretched band
He vowed he would put some to the sword in the morning,
and string up the rest as sport for the birds. But at daybreak
hope returned to the dispirited Geats when they heard the
horn and trumpet of Hygelac following up their track with
a picked body of men.

41

'THE bloody wake of the Swedes and Geats, how each side
joined battle, and the slaughter where they had fought, was
plain to see. The veteran leader Ongentheow, much dis-
turbed, withdrew a short way with his followers into his
stronghold. He knew of Hygelac's skill and prowess and
doubted whether he was strong enough to beat off the raid-
ing army and defend his gold, wife, and children from the
freebooters. So the old man retreated behind his fortifica-
tions. But pursuit was given to the Swedes; and when the
Geats charged the rampart, the banner of Hygelac overran
the fort.

'The sword's edge brought white-haired Ongentheow
to bay, until he was completely at the mercy of Eofor. The
brother of Eofor, Wulf son of Wonred, struck Ongen-
theow so fierce a blow with his weapon that blood spurted

from the veins beneath the hair. Yet the Swedish king was
not in the least dismayed, but wheeled upon his enemy and
quickly repaid the stroke with a much harder one. The
agile Wulf was unable to deal the old man a return thrust
because Ongentheow split the helmet on his head into frag-
ments. He sank to his knees, streaming with blood. But al-
though felled to the ground and badly hurt, his end was not
yet, for he later recovered. As his brother dropped, Eofor,
Hygelac's valiant retainer, shore through the helmet and
shield of Ongentheow with his sword. The king fell
wounded to death. Now that the fight was won there were
many who quickly lifted up Wulf and bandaged his wound.
Meanwhile Eofor stripped Ongentheow of his corselet,
sword, and helmet. He carried the old man's armour to
Hygelac, who accepted the spoils and promised him, as was
proper, a public reward. Hygelac kept his word when he
reached home, and rewarded Eofor and Wulf with im-
mense treasure for that battle. He gave each of them land
and treasure worth 100,000 sceattas,[24] and no one in the
world could resent his presenting them with such gifts
when they had been so bravely won. In addition, Hygelac
gave his only daughter in marriage to Eofor, to grace his
house and as a pledge of friendship.

'That is the feud, and those are the grounds of hatred, on
account of which the Swedes, I have not the least doubt,
are going to attack us as soon as they hear of the death of
our king, who up till now has defended against all comers
our lands and wealth, and our fighting-men when chief-
tains were falling; who furthered the happiness of his
people, and over and above this performed heroic deeds.
Now the best we can do is to make haste to look upon our
king where he lies, and carry him who gave us gold to his
funeral pyre. Nor shall only part of this wealth be con-
sumed with the hero, for there is a hoard of treasure, an

incalculable amount of gold won at terrible cost, and rings which, in the end, he paid for with his own life – these must the flames lick up, and fire cover over. No man shall wear an ornament in his memory, and no beautiful woman a necklet about her throat; but stripped of finery, and in dejection, she must tread not once but many times the paths of exile, now that the hero has done with happiness, laughter, and delight. For this the finger must grasp and the hand lift up many a cold spear in the morning. Music of the harp will not awake the heroes. But the black raven flapping over the dead shall be voluble, and tell the eagle of its luck at dinner, when along with the wolf it plundered the slain.'

Thus the soldier told the bad news, giving the facts without distortion. The whole company arose, and sadly, with tears falling, went to Eagles' Ness to see the spectacle. They found him who in the past had given them gold dead upon the ground, on his final bed. The hero's last day had come. The king of the Geats had perished nobly. They had already seen the weird and loathsome Worm that lay stretched out on the ground before them. Fearful, glittering, scorched with fire, the Dragon measured fifty feet where it lay. At night it used to have the freedom of the air before swooping down into its den; but now lay stone dead, its inhabiting of the barrow at an end. Goblets, flagons, dishes, and rich swords lay beside it, eaten with rust, as they had lain buried in the bosom of the earth for a thousand years. For the vast golden heritage of the ancients had been secured by a spell. No one might lay a finger on the treasure-house unless God Himself, true lord of victories and protector of men, allowed the hoard to be unsealed by a man of His own choice – whoever He thought fit.

42

IT was manifest that things had not gone well with the Dragon which had wrongfully kept the treasure hidden in the barrow. It had killed a great hero, but this feud had been grimly expiated. It is strange in what places a hero may have to meet his end, once the time is up when he may live among kinsmen in his hall. This was true for Beowulf when he set out to find and fight the guardian of the treasure-hoard. He himself did not know what was to bring about his death. For the princes who placed their treasure there had pronounced a solemn curse on it which was to last until doomsday: that whoever rifled the place should be guilty of sin, shut up in dwelling-places of devils, bound in bonds of hell, and tormented with evil. Yet up till then Beowulf had never looked greedily upon their treasure of cursed gold.[25]

Wiglaf son of Weohstan exclaimed, 'Often many have to suffer from the choice of one, as has happened to us. We could not give our king and protector any good advice, or persuade him not to approach the guardian of the treasure-hoard, but let the creature alone go on living in its den till the world's end. Beowulf held to his destiny: the grimly won treasure-hoard lies open. Harsh was the doom that led our king here!

'While I had the chance I entered and saw all the treasures of the vault. My passage into the barrow was by no means easily won. I hastily grabbed a great bundle of treasure into my hands and dragged it here to my king. He was still alive and conscious, and with his wits about him. In spite of his pain he spoke of a good many things; and he commanded me to salute you and ask you to build a tumulus on the site of his funeral pyre: a great and splendid one befitting his exploits, for as long as he ruled his kingdom he was the most renowned hero in the world. Let us hasten once more to look upon the marvellous spectacle in the vault and find the mass of treasure. I will show you where you can gaze upon a heap of rings and broad gold at close quarters. Let the bier be made ready the moment we come out, and then let us carry our beloved king to the place where he must rest long in the keeping of God.'

Then Wiglaf gave orders to the soldiers, householders, and chieftains, to fetch timber for the hero's pyre.

'Now let black flames shoot up and fire swallow this prince of fighting-men, who so often faced a rain of steel, when sped by bowstrings a gale of arrows hurtled over sheltering shields, and the feather-flighted shaft did its work, driving home the barb.'

Wiglaf next summoned seven of the king's best men from the host, and with them entered the unfriendly vault. The leading man carried a burning torch in his hand. When the troops saw the bulk of the treasure lying mouldering and unguarded in the vault, no lots needed to be drawn as to who should loot the hoard; no one had the least scruple over pillaging the valuables as quickly as possible. They heaved the Worm over the cliff as well, and let the waves bear away and the sea cover the guardian of the treasure. A quite incalculable amount of twisted gold was loaded upon a wagon; and the old king was carried up to Hronesness.

43

THE people of the Geats prepared for Beowulf, as he had asked of them, a splendid pyre hung about with helmets, shields, and shining corselets. Then, mourning, the soldiers

laid their loved and illustrious prince in the midst. Upon
the hill the men-at-arms lit a gigantic funeral fire. Black
wood-smoke whirled over the conflagration; the roar of
flames mixed with the noise of weeping, until the furious
draught subsided and the white-hot body crumbled to
pieces. Sadly they complained of their grief and of the
death of their king. A Geat woman [26] with braided hair
keened a dirge in Beowulf's memory, repeating again and
again that she feared bad times were on the way, with
bloodshed, terror, captivity, and shame. Heaven swallowed
up the smoke.

Upon the headland the Geats erected a broad, high tumu-
lus, plainly visible to distant seamen. In ten days they com-
pleted the building of the hero's beacon. Round his ashes
they built the finest vault that their most skilful men could
devise. Within the barrow they placed collars, brooches,
and all the trappings which they had plundered from the
treasure-hoard. They buried the gold and left that princely
treasure to the keeping of earth, where it yet remains, as
useless to men as it was before.

Then twelve chieftains, all sons of princes, rode round
the barrow lamenting their loss, speaking of their king, re-
citing an elegy, and acclaiming the hero. They praised his
manhood and extolled his heroic deeds. It is right that men
should pay homage to their king with words, and cherish
him in their hearts, when he has taken leave of the body. So
the Geats who had shared his hall mourned the death of
their lord, and said that of all kings he was the gentlest and
most gracious of men, the kindest to his people and the
most desirous of renown.

NOTES

1. This Beowulf, an ancestor of the Danish Royal House, is not the hero of the poem and is only once again mentioned.
2. See Appendix: *Sutton Hoo and Beowulf*.
3. The reference, with its typically heavy Anglo-Saxon irony, is to Grendel.
4. This passage is also ironic. Grendel had killed thirty of Hrothgar's followers. Therefore, according to Germanic custom (and to Anglo-Saxon law), he owed Hrothgar *wergild* (man-gold, payment, i.e. blood-money) for them.
5. Because this sentence has been held to be out of place here, suggestions have been made for transferring it elsewhere. The real difficulty is whether the throne is God's or Hrothgar's. I incline to the latter view. Grendel has visited the hall for so long that the poet ironically visualized him trying to approach the king's throne, where the treasures were dispensed, as if he were a retainer. In either case Grendel is prevented from approaching the throne because, as a descendant of Cain (the first murderer) he is cut off from God's love.
6. There are textual difficulties here. The alternative interpretations would make Beowulf listen to heroic deeds, not tell of them.
7. The text admits of different interpretations. Beowulf's apparent inactivity until actually attacked may be a survival from earlier folk-tales (see R. W. Chambers, *Introduction to Beowulf*, pp. 63-4).
8. Weapons of good quality were highly prized and handed down from father to son. Professor Wrenn notes: 'It seems that the art of making good weapons deteriorated from the fourth to the sixth centuries, so that good weapons were traditionally treated somewhat like a Stradivarius violin.'
9. The Danish chieftain is paying Beowulf the highest of compliments by comparing him to one of the greatest of Germanic

heroes. Strictly speaking, Sigemund's dragon-slaying exploits which are recounted here correspond to those of his son Sigurðr in the *Volsungasaga*. Sigurðr killed a dragon which guarded a treasure; he carried it off, but there was a curse on it which finally brought about his doom. A parallel with Beowulf's own fate is thus introduced. The choice of this particular story to exalt Beowulf in his first moment of triumph is a good example of the poet's allusive use of ironic tragic anticipation.

10. Heremod, an unknown Danish king of evil memory, is here referred to for the first time. Throughout the poem he is used as an example of the worst type of leader, and his bad qualities and disastrous reign provide a foil to Beowulf. Unlike the latter, who (as we are told further on) was not much thought of to start with, yet became the greatest of heroes, Heremod's career began with every promise; but owing to his tyrannous and parsimonious behaviour – which alienated him from his people – concluded ignominiously.

11. To a Germanic hero no higher praise could be given.

12. Apart from the reference to the burning of Heorot at the beginning of the poem, this is the first of several foreboding allusions to the subsequent history of the Danes. Hrothulf was the son of Hrothgar's younger brother Halga. From the *Historica Danica* of Saxo Grammaticus and other sources, it is clear that after the death of Hrothgar, Hrothulf began a civil war in Denmark during which he killed Hrothgar's son and heir, Hrethric, and seized the throne.

13. See Appendix: *Sutton Hoo and Beowulf*.

14. 'The Finn Episode' has probably caused more dissension than any other part of *Beowulf*. Since the story was certainly not new to the poet's audience, he was able to treat it in an allusive manner; the result would have been clear to them, but it is not so to us. However, we also possess a fragment of a lay on the same subject. The forty-eight lines of 'The Finnsburg Fragment' were discovered by George Hickes, a seventeenth-century scholar, on a single leaf in a volume of homilies in the library of Lambeth Palace. The original MS has been lost, but Hickes transcribed the text and published it in his *Linguarum*

Vett. Septentrionalium Thesaurus (1705). Since this Fragment places its emphasis on the fight itself instead of the tragedy resulting from the fight (which is the subject of the 'Finn Episode' in *Beowulf*) it helps us to fill out the earlier part of the tale. It may be useful, therefore, if I give an outline of the story as I see it.

According to the 'Finnsburg Fragment' a band of sixty men (two of whom are named Guthlaf and Ordlaf) under the leadership of Hnaef are attacked before daybreak in the hall of Finn. It is implied, but not made explicit, that this attack was a treacherous one. They fight without loss against their enemies for five days. Here the 'Finnsburg Fragment' comes to an end in the middle of a line.

By a curious coincidence, the 'Finn Episode' in *Beowulf* begins at almost exactly the point where the 'Finnsburg Fragment' breaks off. In the 'Finn Episode' I take the main sequence of events to be as follows:

A party of Danes, under Hnaef, is attacked by the followers of Finn, the king of the Jutes and Frisians. Finn is married to a Danish princess, Hildeburh, who is the sister of Hnaef. As well as Hnaef, the son of Finn and Hildeburh is killed in the battle. On the death of Hnaef, his second-in-command Hengest takes over the leadership of the Danes. Finn's army has suffered such heavy losses that he cannot dislodge the Danish remnant from the hall. So Finn offers the Danes a peace treaty. The peace treaty provides for the hall to be shared equally by the Frisians and Jutes and the Danes, and for the Danes to receive their fair share when Finn distributed treasure to his followers. As Finn was responsible for the death of Hnaef, and it was regarded as a dishonour to follow the killer of one's own leader, the treaty specially provided for the punishment by death of any of Finn's men who might reopen the feud by reminding Hnaef's former retainers of their equivocal position. When the treaty has been ratified the dead on both sides are burned on a funeral pyre. Hengest and his men spend the winter in Finn's stronghold. But Hengest is unable to keep from thoughts of vengeance. One of the Danes reminds him of his duty to avenge Hnaef by laying a sword across his knees. Then Guthlaf and Oslaf (perhaps the Guthlaf and Ordlaf of the 'Finnsburg Fragment') complain bitterly and blame Hengest, upon which he can no longer control himself but contrives a revenge in the course of which Finn is killed in his own hall. The Danes then loot the stronghold, and carry Hildeburh back with them to Denmark.

Textually, this interpretation demands:

(a) that the 'sudden disaster' – the initial attack which provoked all the fighting – befel Hnaef, and not Finn's men;

(b) that Finn and not Hengest proposed the truce to the first battle (the 'they' and 'them' of the Old English text is ambiguous);

(c) that the text does not name the sword given to Hengest as a symbol of vengeance. 'Hunlafing' is therefore the name of a warrior and *hilde-leoman* merely a kenning for 'sword';

(d) that Guthlaf and Ordlaf implied Hengest was to blame for not exacting vengeance for Hnaef. Since I here supply an object to the verb used, the passage could mean that, provoking Finn to action by some (unspecified) complaint, they caused him to break the truce agreed earlier.

15. This raid is mentioned four times in the poem and we can piece together the following outline of events:

Hygelac and his fleet raided Frisian territory on the Lower Rhine, part of the Frankish empire. They obtained much booty and the fleet had just started on its homeward journey when a strong Frankish force attacked. Hygelac was defeated and killed. Beowulf slew Daeghrefn, a champion and standard-bearer of the Hugas (another name for the Franks), and escaped by swimming to Geatland, there to become regent and later king.

The four references in *Beowulf* each stress a different aspect of the battle:

(a) line 1202 ff., p. 55. Stresses Hygelac's rash action in undertaking the raid, and his defeat.

(b) line 2354 ff., p. 82. Mentions the name of the Hetware (a Frankish tribe from the Rhine valley, allies of the Merovingians) as Hygelac's opponents, and underlines Beowulf's prowess, and his escape by swimming.

(c) line 2501 ff., p. 86. Describes Beowulf's hand-to-hand struggle with Daeghrefn, champion of the Hugas.

(d) line 2910 ff., p. 95. Mentions the Hugas as well as the Hetware, and stresses the resulting enmity between Merovingians and Geats.

From this account it will appear that the poet was adopting his usual allusive technique and assumed knowledge of these events on the part of his audience.

Hygelac's raid can be dated on historical grounds as having occurred about A.D. 521. The incident is mentioned in Frankish sources, the *Historica Francorum* of Gregory of Tours (composed about 575) and the anonymous *Liber Historiae Francorum* (about 727), which mentions the Hetware. Both accounts give a Latin form of Hygelac's name and refer to him as a Dane. But an eighth-century collection of stories, the *Liber Monstrorum*, gives the English form of the name and calls him a Geat, as in *Beowulf*; it also says that his bones were preserved at the mouth of the Rhine, where the battle took place (a detail not mentioned in the poem). The *Liber Monstrorum* was probably written in England and suggests that Hygelac was known to the English apart from *Beowulf*. The fact that this part of *Beowulf* is based on historical fact raises the question of the authenticity of the other sections, e.g. the wars between the Swedes and Geats. Professor Wrenn has an excellent discussion on pp. 47–9 of his edition of *Beowulf*. See also Whitelock, *The Audience of Beowulf*, pp. 38–55.

16. The word which was formerly translated as the proper name 'Modthrytho' is now thought to be a noun meaning 'arrogance', and the abrupt transition from Hygd to an unnamed queen of entirely different disposition is explained by the assumption of a lost passage between the two halves of line 1931. But in view of the possible Mercian origin of the poem, it may be that the poet was dragging in a reference to the contemporary King Offa II of Mercia, whose famous ancestor, Offa the Great, flourished on the Continent in the fourth cen-

tury and is mentioned in the Old English poem *Widsith*. This was the Offa who tamed his overbearing queen Thryth. (See Whitelock, *The Audience of Beowulf*, pp. 57–64.) The translation compromises in an attempt to retain some continuity.

17. This is my rendering of 'freoðu-webbe' ('weaver of peace'), which is a kenning for 'lady' because the marriage of a princess to the leader of another nation was often intended to cement the friendship of the two peoples. That at least was the ideal. A few pages further on we hear of the marriage of Freawaru to Ingeld, which failed to settle the Danish–Heathobard feud.

18. An enormous glove is a characteristic property of trolls in Old Norse legends.

19. Two pages of the *Beowulf* manuscript are very badly damaged. The first begins here and introduces the Dragon story. The second includes the final lines of the poem. It has been suggested that the part of the poem dealing with the Dragon fight was at one time bound separately and that these two outside leaves suffered from excessive handling. They also show some discoloration and blurring which may have been caused by the application of some chemical (perhaps intended to 'freshen up' the letters) and the effect of damp. Modern methods of examining manuscripts (e.g. the use of the ultra-violet lamp) have enabled editors to reconstruct some of the doubtful words. The most important of these discoveries are due to J. C. Pope (see note 26). Wrenn's edition of *Beowulf* includes the recent restorations, and the present translation is based on it, introducing as few unauthenticated readings as seems consistent with good sense.

20. This famous passage (sometimes called 'The Survivor's Lament') is one of the most characteristic and impressive examples of Anglo-Saxon elegiac poetry.

21. It was usual (especially in Scandinavia) for men of good birth to place their sons in the hands of a foster-father in order to be educated.

22. An accidental manslaughter of this kind was punishable. But the point is that Hrethel cannot fulfil the duty of avenging his

son, since to do so would mean lifting his hand against his own kin.

23. The case of Herebeald suggests to Beowulf another tragic instance of the kind of situation when no vengeance can be exacted. It was a principle of Anglo-Saxon law that no revenge could be taken for an executed criminal. This is an elegiac passage reminiscent of 'The Survivor's Lament'.

24. No one knows the real value of the sceatt (an Anglo-Saxon coin) in the eighth century. Its value varied according to the place and date. Professor Wrenn guesses the combined value of the land and treasure at £400 in Anglo-Saxon money. What this would be worth today it is impossible to say.

25. A much-disputed passage, largely because this is the only known instance of the Old English word gold-hwaet, and the fact that the Old English est can have various senses. It is also uncertain whether the 'owner' refers to God or to the original depositor of the treasure. The translation adopted seems to suit the context best, but other possible renderings would be:

(a) Yet Beowulf had never before looked too eagerly upon its owner's treasure rich in gold.

(b) Not before had Beowulf beheld more fully the gold-abounding grace of the Lord (i.e. this was the biggest prize of gold he had ever won).

(c) Unless God's grace had first more readily favoured those eager for gold. (This involves an emendation.)

26. The hitherto quite illegible word before 'meowle' ('woman') was recently deciphered by J. C. Pope. His reading is 'Geatisc meowle' ('The Geat woman'), and some scholars have thought that this phrase must therefore refer to Hygd, the widow of Hygelac, and that the mention of her as leading Beowulf's funeral lamentations proves that Beowulf must have married her. Such speculation, however, does not seem very profitable; and there is the point that Hygd was, in any case, Beowulf's aunt by marriage.

APPENDIX I

The Author, Manuscript, and Bibliography of Beowulf

WE do not know who the author of *Beowulf* was. A nineteenth-century scholar, John Earle, once made a gallant attempt to identify him with Hygeberht, an archbishop of Lichfield who lived in the eighth century. But the poem is generally supposed to have been written by a contemporary of the Venerable Bede (who died in 735) at the time when Anglo-Saxon learning and literature were at their zenith in Northumbria. There is, however, no direct evidence. Some think that *Beowulf* may have been composed somewhat later than this, perhaps by a poet at the court of King Offa (who died in 796). Offa, the king of Mercia who built Offa's Dyke, was one of the greatest and most powerful Anglo-Saxon monarchs before the birth of King Alfred. The idea that *Beowulf* might have been written by a poet at the Mercian court seems to be supported by a eulogy about Offa the Angle (the king of Mercia's namesake and legendary ancestor) which is to be found in the poem. This eulogy is rather abruptly (unless, as has been suggested, a few lines have been lost) hauled in by means of an anecdote whose relevance to the main theme of the poem seems otherwise obscure. Concerning Offa the Angle, the poet of Beowulf says that he was 'the best of kings the wide world over ... a notable soldier, ruled his native land wisely, and was famous everywhere for his victories and his generosity'. Such an oblique compliment would be a typical piece of poetic flattery. However, it can only be safely asserted that the poem of *Beowulf* must have been composed in either Mercia or Northumbria, not earlier than the end of the seventh century nor much later than the beginning of the ninth.*

The text of *Beowulf* derives from a single manuscript now in the British Museum. This manuscript was made about the year 1000,

* Early in the ninth century the Viking invasions which all but destroyed Anglo-Saxon civilization began to get under way.

two or three centuries later than the probable date of the composition of the poem. It is the work of two scribes, whose scripts and spellings are quite distinct. In 1563 this manuscript appears to have been in the hands of Laurence Nowell, Dean of Lichfield, one of the first students of Old English. He may have been responsible for its preservation, because in his day, the time following the dissolution of the monasteries, a vast number of ancient manuscripts were destroyed. But in any case the *Beowulf* MS came into the possession of Sir Robert Bruce Cotton (*d.* 1631) and remained in his famous library until, a century after his death, there was an unlucky fire which wholly destroyed a hundred volumes and severely damaged ninety others. That containing *Beowulf* was badly scorched, especially about the edges, some of which crumbled away before the book could be properly rebound. Thus a good many words and in some cases whole passages of the poem were lost altogether. Fortunately the Danish scholar G. J. Thorkelin came to England in 1786. He had one copy of the text made by a professional scribe and made another himself. In this way many letters and words which have since disappeared from the manuscript have been preserved.

Thorkelin's interest in *Beowulf* was due to a misapprehension. At the end of the eighteenth century there was a movement among Danish scholars for the preservation of Danish antiquities. *Beowulf* had found a place in Humphrey Wanley's famous *Catalogue of Anglo-Saxon Manuscripts*, which was published in 1705. (This is the first mention of the poem anywhere.) Wanley vaguely and wrongly described it as being about the wars of the Swedes with the Danes; however, the description led Thorkelin to get *Beowulf* transcribed, and to spend many years preparing an edition of it. But when the English bombarded Copenhagen in 1807 it was nearly lost, because Thorkelin's house was burnt and his edition destroyed. Fortunately both transcripts of the poem were saved; and the Danish Privy Councillor, John Bülow, persuaded Thorkelin to start all over again. In 1815 Thorkelin brought out the first printed edition of *Beowulf*, with a parallel translation done in Latin.

The first English edition of the poem did not appear until 1833.

This was the work of J. M. Kemble, a Cambridge don, son of the famous actor Charles Kemble. In 1837 he published the first translation of *Beowulf* into English. But by the end of the nineteenth century the bibliography of *Beowulf* had already become formidable; the poem had been edited by at least a dozen scholars, Danish, German, and English, and translated many times. Almost every conceivable theory about its meaning, date, and authorship was aired, sometimes giving rise to scholarly feuds as implacable as any of those described in the poem.

It should not be forgotten that the study of Anglo-Saxon literature is comparatively new. While the *Aeneid*, for instance, has been in the hands of poets and learned men more or less since it was first written, for practical purposes *Beowulf*, 800 years its junior, has been available for little more than a century. Its very existence was generally unknown until 1705, and its text remained unpublished until 1815. Much hard spadework had to be done by the early editors and translators. Even today, in the present state of Anglo-Saxon studies, there are many passages in *Beowulf* whose exact significance remains obscure, ambiguous, or impossible to elucidate. So it is perhaps not very surprising that in spite of a vast crop of editions and translations, plus a daunting library of books about it, *Beowulf* in the nineteenth century was hardly ever seriously considered as a work of art. The editor of the *Oxford Book of English Verse* referred to it as 'small beer'. Only within the last twenty years has there been any sustained attempt to size it up as a poem, or to prise it from the vice of philologists, historians, mythologists, and the rest, whose opinions concerning the literary merit of the object of their labours have often been scathing. The temptation to regard *Beowulf* as a quarry for almost everything except its poetry was however a strong one. The oldest epic in any non-classical European tongue, it has no real parallel in any literature; the circumstances of its survival were almost entirely haphazard; and, finally, its construction and method are unique. But it is owing to the patience and labour of specialists, especially nineteenth-century scholars like Grundtvig, Kemble, Thorpe, Grein, Heyne, Earle, Wyatt, and Clark-Hall, that we know as much as we do about *Beowulf*, and can interpret and translate its text so much more accurately than its heroic pioneer, G. J. Thorkelin.

The two latest editions of *Beowulf* are those of C. L. Wrenn (London, 1958) and E. Van Kirk Dobbie, *The Anglo-Saxon Poetic Records*, volume V. But the famous editions of Klaeber, especially his 3rd edition of 1951, are fundamental to any serious study of the text. The more advanced student of *Beowulf* should not neglect those of A. J. Wyatt and R. W. Chambers (Cambridge, 1914) nor Else von Schaubert's revision of the German Heyne-Schücking edition (Paderborn, 1958–9). Of fairly recent critical work, the most particularly to be recommended are R. W. Chambers's *Introduction to Beowulf* (3rd Edition, with Supplement by C. L. Wrenn, Cambridge, 1959); W. W. Lawrence's *Beowulf and the Epic Tradition* (Cambridge, Mass., 1928); J. R. R. Tolkien's notable essay *Beowulf: the Monsters and the Critics* (Proceedings of the British Academy, vol. xxii, 1936); A. Bonjour's *The Digressions in Beowulf* (Oxford, 1950); Dorothy Whitelock's *The Audience of Beowulf* (Oxford, 1951); A. G. Brodeur's *The Art of Beowulf* (Berkeley, 1959); *Studies in Old English Literature in Honor of A. G. Brodeur*, ed. S. Greenfield (1963); and K. Sisam's *The Structure of Beowulf* (Oxford, 1965).

Those who wish to know more of the life and times of the Anglo-Saxons will find a very readable account in Dorothy Whitelock's *The Beginnings of English Society* (London, 1952; published in the Pelican series) and a full and detailed treatment in Sir Frank Stenton's *Anglo-Saxon England* (2nd edition, Oxford, 1947), which is indispensable to any student of early English history.

APPENDIX II

Sutton Hoo and Beowulf

AN important archaeological discovery made in 1939 at Sutton Hoo on the tidal estuary of the river Deben in Suffolk has substantially contributed to the understanding of certain parts of *Beowulf*. In the tallest of a group of mounds were found remains of a ship burial. The timbers of the ship had perished, but the splendid grave goods were discovered practically intact. These treasures are now in the British Museum. The best account of the find is in the Appendix by R. Bruce-Mitford to the 3rd edition (1952) of R. H. Hodgkin's *History of the Anglo-Saxons*. The British Museum pamphlet, *The Sutton Hoo Ship-Burial* (1951), is also a good general treatment. Both contain plates and diagrams.

Perhaps the most remarkable finds in the grave are the sword, shield, and helmet; an object identified as a battle-standard; a golden harness with carved belt-buckle; a harp (probably of the type used to accompany poems like *Beowulf*); ceremonial drinking-horns (presumably like those used in Heorot); the decorated lid of a purse; and, from the purse itself, gold Frankish coins which have been dated 650–70. Several silver objects originate from the eastern Mediterranean, and designs and inscriptions on some of these point to Christian owners. Hanging bowls, implying contact with Ireland or Celtic West Britain, are further evidence of the range covered by the deposit. The grave is almost certainly that of a ruler and is in fact situated only four miles from the residence of the East Saxon kings at Rendlesham.

There is, however, no trace of a body. The theory usually advanced is that it is a cenotaph and that the body of the king commemorated was either buried elsewhere or lost. A further difficulty is that the East Anglian dynasty at this period was predominantly Christian, and Sutton Hoo is a burial in a pagan cemetery. Bruce-Mitford suggests two possible solutions. One is that we have a monument to a pagan ruler whose Christian relatives placed the silver pieces mentioned above in the grave for the good of his soul. This would fit Aelfhere (*d.* 655), who perished fighting in Yorkshire and whose body was probably washed away by floods – but his was an inglorious reign of only one year, scarcely worth such a commemoration. The other solution suggests a public monument, in the pagan tradition, set up to a Christian king. In this event the most likely ruler is Anna (*d.* 654), a distinguished Christian king who ruled the East Anglians for about fifteen years. Writing in *Antiquity* for 1948, Sune Lindqvist argues that the Church would probably not hinder new converts from furnishing their dead with such a magnificent collection of grave-goods as might suggest a purely pagan burial to modern eyes.

All this probably happened less than a century before the composition of *Beowulf*. The poem opens with an account of the obsequies of Scyld Scefing. In the light of the Sutton Hoo discovery, the splendour of the treasures surrounding the dead Scyld is seen to be no mere poetical exaggeration; the battle-standard (line 47 of *Beowulf*) is probably paralleled here. But a sailing-ship bore Scyld's body out to sea, unlike the Sutton Hoo boat, which had no mast and was propelled by oars, and which was buried in the earth. The account of Beowulf's funeral at the close of the poem smacks, as Professor Wrenn says, of traditions from the heroic age rather than of history proper, and is not greatly illuminated by the findings in Suffolk. In fact, in both cases the poet may have based his descriptions on older accounts of such burials, and, letting his imagination play, have produced verisimilitude rather than exact description.

A more detailed correspondence between Sutton Hoo and *Beowulf* is in the helmet. The helmet in the grave has not the boar-crest described in the poem:

Above their helmets glittered boar-crests of tempered gold keeping watch over the Geats.

but it does show what appear to be gilded boar-images at the ends of the eyebrows, and these may well have performed a similar function. The bronze sheets covering the outer surfaces of the Sutton Hoo helmet appear to have been tinned, giving, at least when new, a shining effect. This, plus the gold and garnets seen elsewhere on the helmet, adds a new meaning to the description in *Beowulf* which speaks of the hero's helmet as 'glistening ... inlaid with gold'. We can also now explain lines 1030–40, since from front to back of the Sutton Hoo helmet runs a strong tube of iron (presumably meant to protect the head below from the full force of a sword-blow) and the outer surface of this tube is inlaid with silver wires – an almost exact correspondence with the description given in the poem:

Round the top of the helmet a projecting rim bound with wires guarded the head in such a way that no sword, however sharp and tough, might cripple the wearer when he joined battle with his enemies.

Finally, the discovery at Sutton Hoo postulates a strong connexion between Sweden and Suffolk before the opening of the Viking period, for these places are the only two in Europe where we find boat-inhumation at this time. The helmet and shield show particularly close parallels in design and detail with Swedish discoveries. It does not seem fanciful, therefore, to compare the connexion between Old English traditions and Swedish history as we see it in *Beowulf*. Lindqvist, indeed, has gone so far as to hazard the guess that the poem itself may have been written to honour the descendants of Wiglaf, who prided themselves on their connexion with the royal house of Sweden.

APPENDIX III
Genealogical Tables

THE DANISH ROYAL HOUSE

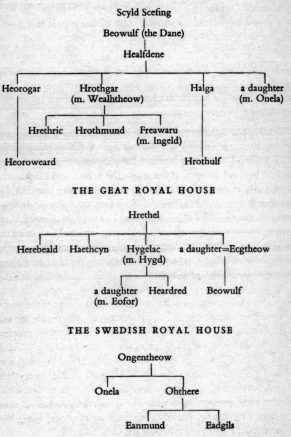

Scyld Scefing

Beowulf (the Dane)

Healfdene

Heorogar — Hrothgar (m. Wealhtheow) — Halga — a daughter (m. Onela)

Hrethric — Hrothmund — Freawaru (m. Ingeld)

Heoroweard

Hrothulf

THE GEAT ROYAL HOUSE

Hrethel

Herebeald — Haethcyn — Hygelac (m. Hygd) — a daughter=Ecgtheow

a daughter (m. Eofor) — Heardred

Beowulf

THE SWEDISH ROYAL HOUSE

Ongentheow

Onela — Ohthere

Eanmund — Eadgils

GLOSSARY OF PROPER NAMES

ABEL The son of Adam, in the Book of Genesis, murdered by his brother Cain.

AELFHERE An ancestor of Weohstan and Wiglaf.

AESCHERE Elder brother of Yrmenlaf; Hrothgar's old comrade-in-arms and counsellor, killed by Grendel's mother.

BEANSTAN Father of Breca.

BEOWULF There are two Beowulfs in the poem. The first, Beowulf the Dane, is son of Scyld Scefing and grandfather of the Danish king Hrothgar. The other Beowulf, the hero of the poem, is a Geat, son of Ecgtheow and nephew of Hygelac, the Geat king. Later he succeeded to the Geat throne.

BRECA Son of Beanstan and king of the Brondings, with whom Beowulf had his famous swimming-contest.

BRONDINGS Name of an unidentified tribe: see BRECA

BROSINGS Perhaps an error for Brisings, the tribe who in old Norse legend made a magic necklace for the goddess Freyja.

CAIN The eldest son of Adam, in the Book of Genesis; murderer of Abel. In the poem he is the legendary forebear of the monster Grendel.

DAEGHREFN Champion and standard-bearer of the Franks; killed by Beowulf when Hygelac invaded the Netherlands.

DANES In the original, several cognomens are used for the people always referred to as 'Danes' in this translation. Some are self-explanatory, e.g. 'North-Danes'; some probably supplied heroic colouring, e.g. 'Bright-Danes', 'Spear-Danes', 'Ring-(i.e. treasure-) Danes'. They are sometimes called *Scyldings* after their ruling family, and twice 'the friends of Ing' a mythical god, mentioned in Tacitus, whose place in later mythology may have been usurped by Scyld. The choice of any one of these names by the poet probably has little significance, being dictated chiefly by the demands of the alliteration.

DENMARK The Danish kingdom embraced the southern tip of Sweden as well as Denmark proper.

EADGILS A Swedish prince, younger son of Ohthere, and brother of Eanmund, with whom he rebelled against their uncle Onela. Later, with Beowulf's assistance, he invaded Sweden, killed Onela, and became king.

EANMUND A Swedish prince, elder son of Ohthere, and brother of Eadgils; killed by Weohstan, father of Wiglaf.

ECGLAF The father of Unferth.

ECGTHEOW The father of Beowulf the Geat; married the only daughter of Hrethel, the king of the Geats and the father of Hygelac.

ECGWELA An unknown Danish king.

EOFOR A Geat, son of Wonred and brother of Wulf; killed the Swedish king Ongentheow.

EOMER Son of Offa.

EORMENRIC The historical king of the Ostrogoths. Also mentioned in the Anglo-Saxon poem of *Widsith*.

FINN King of the Frisians, and also ruler of the Jutes; son of Folcwalda and husband of Hildeburh, the sister of Hnaef.

FITELA Son, nephew, and companion of Sigemund.

FOLCWALDA Father of Finn.

FRANKS The most powerful people in Western Europe in the eighth century, ruling most of France, Germany, and the Netherlands.

FREAWARU Daughter of Hrothgar king of the Danes; married Ingeld, prince of the Heathobards.

FRIESLAND The land of the Frisians (east and north of the Zuyder Zee).

FRISIANS The tribe inhabiting the land round the Zuyder Zee. Under the domination of the Franks. Attacked by Hygelac of the Geats. Followers of Finn.

FRODA The king of the Heathobards and father of Ingeld.

GARMUND Father of Offa.

GEATS Beowulf's tribe. They lived in southern Sweden and were enemies of the Swedes, who probably overthrew them during the sixth century (after the death of Beowulf).

GIFTHAS The Gepidae, an East Germanic tribe who in the third century emigrated from the Vistula delta to Hungary. They are mentioned in *Widsith*. Since the name in *Beowulf* occurs in close connexion with the Swedes and Geats, the poet seems still to have been thinking of them as inhabitants of the Baltic seaboard.

GRENDEL The monster who ravaged Heorot. He is supposed to have been descended from Cain.

GUTHLAF A Dane; one of Hnaef's and Hengest's followers.

HAERETH Father of Hygelac's wife, Hygd.

HAETHCYN King of the Geats; second son of Hrethel. Accidentally killed his elder brother Herebeald. Killed by the Swedish king Ongentheow at the battle of Ravenswood.

HALGA Youngest son of the Danish king Healfdene.

HAMA A Germanic hero, also mentioned in *Widsith*.

HEALFDENE A Danish king, son of Beowulf the Dane, and father of Hrothgar.

HEARDRED King of the Geats; son of Hygelac. He was killed by the Swedish king Onela and succeeded by Beowulf.

HEATHOBARDS An unidentified Germanic tribe, enemies of the Danes. Hrothgar tried unsuccessfully to settle the feud by marrying his daughter to the Heathobard leader, Ingeld.

HEATHOLAF A Wilfing, killed by Ecgtheow the father of Beowulf.

HELMINGS The tribe of Wealhtheow, Hrothgar's queen. In *Widsith*, Helm is a king of the Wylfings, a Germanic tribe living on the southern shore of the Baltic.

HEMMING A kinsman of Offa and Garmund.

HENGEST A Danish chieftain, who took over the command of the Danes after Finn's men had killed Hnaef.

HEOROGAR Son of Healfdene, and elder brother of the Danish king Hrothgar.

HEOROT The hall which Hrothgar built. Its actual site can almost certainly be identified with Leire in Zeeland. The name means 'hart'. It was burnt down during the Danish–Heathobard feud.

HEOROWEARD Son of the Danish king Heorogar and nephew of Hrothgar.

HEREBEALD A Geat prince, eldest son of Hrethel king of the Geats and brother of Haethcyn and Hygelac; killed accidentally by Haethcyn.

HEREMOD An unknown Danish king, mentioned as a stock example of a bad type of ruler.

HETWARE A Frankish tribe living on the Lower Rhine. The actual tribe who defeated Hygelac during the latter's raid.

HILDEBURH A Danish princess, the daughter of Hoc and wife of Finn king of the Frisians and ruler of the Jutes; sister of the Danish leader Hnaef, who was killed by Finn's men.

HNAEF A Danish chieftain, killed by Finn's men during a battle; brother of Hildeburh, the wife of Finn.

HOC Father of Hildeburh.

HONDSCIOH A Geat, one of Beowulf's followers, who was killed by Grendel in Heorot.

HREOSNABURGH A hill in the Geat country, where the Swedes attacked the Geats after the death of their king Hrethel.

HRETHEL A Geat king, father of Hygelac and grandfather of Beowulf. He died of grief because one of his sons, Herebeald, was accidentally killed by another son, Haethcyn.

HRETHRIC Son and heir of Hrothgar. Later killed by Hrothulf when the latter usurped the Danish throne after the death of Hrothgar.

HRONESNESS 'The whale's promontory' – a headland on the Geat coast where Beowulf's funeral tumulus was built.

HROTHGAR The king of the Danes; son of Healfdene, brother of Heorogar and Halga; husband of Wealhtheow and father of Hrethric, Hrothmund, and Freawaru.

HROTHMUND Son of Hrothgar king of the Danes.

HROTHULF Nephew to the Danish king Hrothgar, and son of Hrothgar's younger brother Halga. From Scandinavian sources it is known that after Hrothgar's death Hrothulf usurped the Danish throne, and killed Hrethric, Hrothgar's son and heir.

HRUNTING Unferth's sword, which he lent to Beowulf for his fight with Grendel's mother.

HUNLAFING A Danish follower of Hnaef and Hengest.

HYGD The wife of Hygelac king of the Geats; daughter of Haereth and mother of Heardred. Her name means 'Prudence'.

HYGELAC Beowulf's uncle, and king of the Geats; husband of Hygd and father of Heardred.

INGELD Prince of the Heathobards; the son of Froda. He married Freawaru, daughter of Hrothgar king of the Danes.

JUTES Originally the Jutes probably lived near the Frisians. In the poem Finn keeps a band of Jutes as well as his own Frisians The Jutes later inhabited present-day Jutland in north Denmark. The Anglo-Saxon word for Jute was 'Eote' or 'Yte'. 'Eoten' also means 'giant'.

NAEGLING The name of Beowulf's sword with which he fought the Dragon.

OFFA King of the continental Angles; the husband of Thryth. He was the ancestor of the historical Offa, King of Mercia.

OHTHERE A Swedish prince, son of Ongentheow the Swedish king; brother of Onela, and father of Eanmund and Eadgils.

ONELA A Swedish king, the son of Ongentheow and the brother of Ohthere. He invaded the country of the Geats and killed their king Heardred. Later he was killed by his own nephew Eadgils, when with Beowulf's assistance Eadgils invaded Sweden.

ONGENTHEOW King of the Swedes; father of Onela and Ohthere. He killed the Geat king Haethcyn, and was himself killed by Eofor the Geat at the battle of Ravenswood.

OSLAF A Dane, one of Hnaef's and Hengest's followers.

RAVENSWOOD A forest in Sweden, scene of the battle between the Geats and Swedes, in which the Geat king Haethcyn, and the Swedish king Ongentheow, were killed. The Geats were the victors.

SCANDINAVIA Used of the Danish dominions in the poem, but indicating that the original home of the Danes was in the extreme south of present-day Sweden (Skane).

SCYLD SCEFING The mythological founder of the Danish Royal House. His name means 'son of Sceaf' or, more likely, 'child with the sheaf'; he may originally have been an agriculture c fertility figure.

SIGEMUND A legendary Germanic hero; the son of Waels and

the father and uncle of Fitela. In *Beowulf* Sigemund kills a
dragon; in the *Volsungasaga* and *Nibelungenlied* it is Sigemund's
son Sigurð or Siegfried who is the dragon-slayer.

SWEDES Lived in Central Sweden. In *Beowulf* they are enemies of
the Geats, their southern neighbours. The Swedish kings men-
tioned in the poem are probably historical.

SWERTING An ancestor of Hygelac king of the Geats.

THRYTH The wife of Offa (but see Note 16).

UNFERTH The son of Ecglaf; the 'þyle' (spokesman or orator) of
Hrothgar king of the Danes. He picked a quarrel with Beowulf
on the latter's arrival at Heorot, but afterwards lent him his
sword to fight Grendel's mother.

WAEGMUNDINGS The family of Beowulf the Geat, and of
Wiglaf. Related to the Geat royal house.

WAELS The father of Sigemund.

WEALHTHEOW The wife of Hrothgar king of the Danes, and
mother of Hrethric and Hrothmund.

WELAND The famous legendary Germanic smith and magician.

WENDLAS Possibly to be identified with the Vandals who ulti-
mately settled on the Mediterranean coasts, but on their trek
south probably left settlements in Sweden and Jutland. Wulfgar
(q.v.) probably came from Vendel in Sweden.

WEOHSTAN The father of Wiglaf. He killed Eanmund, the
Swedish prince who was brother of Eadgils who later became
king of Sweden.

WIGLAF The son of Weohstan, kinsman of Beowulf, who came
to the aid of the hero during his fight with the Dragon.

WILFINGS A Germanic tribe, also mentioned in *Widsith*. Their
habitat is uncertain; it may have been on the southern shore of
the Baltic, perhaps the Pomeranian coast.

WITHERGYLD A Heathobard killed in battle with the Danes.

WONRED A Geat, father of Eofor and Wulf.

WULF A Geat, son of Wonred and brother of Eofor, who was
wounded by Ongentheow in the battle of Ravenswood.

WULFGAR A chieftain of the Wendels and an official of the court
of the Danish king Hrothgar.

YRMENLAF Younger brother of Aeschere the Dane.

A selection of books published by Penguin is listed on the following pages.

For a complete list of books available from Penguin in the United States, write to Dept. DG, Penguin Books, 299 Murray Hill Parkway, East Rutherford, New Jersey 07073.

For a complete list of books available from Penguin in Canada, write to Penguin Books Canada Limited, 2801 John Street, Markham, Ontario L3R 1B4.

If you live in the British Isles, write to Dept. EP, Penguin Books Ltd, Harmondsworth, Middlesex.

GEOFFREY OF MONMOUTH
THE HISTORY OF
THE KINGS OF BRITAIN

Translated by Lewis Thorpe

It is difficult to say whether Geoffrey of Monmouth, in writing his famous *Historia Regum Britanniae*, relied more on the old chroniclers or on a gift for romantic invention. Regardless of its merits as history, however, his heroic epic of such half-legendary kings as Cymbeline, Arthur, and Lear enjoyed great popularity and served to inspire Sir Thomas Malory, Edmund Spenser, and William Shakespeare, among other writers. Geoffrey's taste for quaint historical episodes, real or imaginary, and his varied style, which skillfully echoes every mood from quiet description to impassioned oratory, still lend living interest to this twelfth-century chronicle.

CHAUCER
THE CANTERBURY TALES

Translated by Nevill Coghill

The Canterbury Tales stands conspicuous among the great literary achievements of the Middle Ages. Told by a jovial procession of pilgrims—knight, priest, yeoman, miller, and cook—as they ride towards the shrine of Thomas à Becket, they present a picture of a nation taking shape. The tone of this never-resting comedy is, by turns, learned, fantastic, lewd, pious, and ludicrous. 'Here,' as John Dryden said, 'is God's plenty!' Geoffrey Chaucer began his great task in about 1386. This version in modern English, by Nevill Coghill, preserves the freshness and racy vitality of Chaucer's narrative.

SIR GAWAIN AND THE GREEN KNIGHT

Translated by Brian Stone

Sir Gawain and the Green Knight, a poem of 2,500 lines, is the masterpiece of medieval alliterative poetry and was the first poem of the age outside Chaucer's works. In fact, neither Chaucer nor any succeeding poet wrote a narrative poem of such richness. The background is the medieval court and it tells of the adventures of a Christian Knight, although in all probability the origin of the poem was in pagan ritual. Brian Stone's translation is the only easily available complete version in modern English in the original metre.

LAXDAELA SAGA

Translated by Magnus Magnusson and Hermann Palsson

This is the most stirring of all the medieval Icelandic sagas. Its heroine, Gudrun, is forced to marry the best friend of the man she loves and then, in a jealous rage, makes her husband kill her former lover and lose his own life thereby. She is one of the great tragic figures of world literature, and *Laxdaela Saga*, because of its fidelity to Icelandic history, comes close to being a national epic.

GREGORY OF TOURS
THE HISTORY OF THE FRANKS

Translated by Lewis Thorpe

The History of the Franks chronicles the period that led up to and included the twenty-one years that Gregory spent as Bishop of Tours. This Penguin Classics edition contains all ten books of the work, the last seven describing Gregory's own time and especially the quarrels of four of the sons of Lothar I and the machinations of the ruthless Queen Fredegund, third wife of Chilperic. As calamities and disasters unfold, what emerges is no dry historical document but a dramatic picture of France in the sixth century.